A
TIMELESS
CHRISTMAS
AN ENCHANTING TIME TRAVEL ROMANCE

Alexis Stanton

A Timeless Christmas
Copyright @ 2018 Crown Media Family Networks

Print: 978-1-947892-35-4
Ebook: 978-1-947892-34-7

www.hallmarkpublishing.com

TABLE OF CONTENTS

CHAPTER ONE

Megan Turner paused to tuck a wayward strand of her curly hair into her bun, covered by her small cap, before grabbing her brass candlestick from a diminutive, hand-carved table. She hurried toward the foyer, cupping her hand around the candle's flame. It was important to keep it from guttering out as she moved to greet the next wave of visitors to the Whitley-Moran Mansion.

The mansion itself was a thirty-room spectacular, located just a few miles from the little upstate New York town of Cutter Springs, nestled in the Adirondack Mountains. Tourists flocked to the town both for its nearness to the mansion as well as its idyllic country setting. Though Megan had gotten her undergraduate degree from Columbia, she'd quickly returned home to Cutter Springs and its nearby university for her graduate degree in American history.

There was no place better than home.

As she strode down the mansion's long main

corridor, she passed intricately carved door frames, recessed wall panels, and custom-made furnishings. She inhaled deeply, catching the rich, evocative scent from the pine garlands that adorned the walls and doors. A bubble of excitement rose within her.

Christmas was just around the corner, and she couldn't wait. She'd been working as a tour guide at the Whitley-Moran Mansion for two years, and there was something so special about the house during the holiday season. The enormous rooms didn't seem quite so cavernous when each one had a Christmas tree. Each chamber had its own fireplace—a true luxury back when the mansion had been finished in 1902—and swags of evergreen and twinkling glass ornaments decorated each mantel, making every room inviting and cheerful.

It was that special atmosphere that brought visitors by the hundreds to the house during the week leading up to Christmas, including the dozen people now waiting for her in the foyer.

She approached them, noting with happiness that there were men and women, young and old, and people of every color, all here to admire the Christmas cheer in the home of the great Charles Whitley.

"Good afternoon, and merry Christmas," she said brightly as she neared the visitors. She bobbed into a curtsy. "My name is Rosie. I'm the housekeeper. It's my responsibility to keep this ten-bedroom house clean and orderly for Mr. Whitley. It's also my job to keep Mr. Whitley on schedule. He's a very busy man, you know, and *somebody* has to make sure he remembers to eat."

She gave the guests a wink, and they chuckled.

"Now," she said, looking at the children in the group, "does anyone here know who Charles Whitley is?"

A long pause followed. Kids furrowed their brows in thought. One boy of about twelve reached for his pocket, and Megan held up a finger.

"Now, now. I keep seeing our guests with these little devices in their hands, and I don't know what they are, but you can't go looking for answers there."

Naturally, Megan knew exactly what a mobile phone was, but to the character of "Rosie," who knew only the technology of the early twentieth century, such things were strange and baffling.

The boy grinned sheepishly as he lowered his hand.

Finally, a girl of about nine with light brown skin and a mane of fluffy curls raised her hand. When Megan nodded at her, the girl said, "Charles Wilbur Whitley was born in 1870. He was orphaned when he was fourteen, and started working in a steel mill soon after. By the time he was only twenty-one, he'd become rich."

"Exactly," Megan said with an approving smile. "Mr. Whitley amassed a fortune through patenting improvements to the steel milling process, making him the late nineteenth century equivalent of our young tech billionaires. He became one of the country's most wealthy and influential men through his steel empire and technological brilliance."

She gestured to the vaulted ceiling in the foyer.

"He built this house in 1902 as a gift to his fiancée, Eliza. Mr. Whitley spared no expense when building his country estate, including hiring architects from France, as well as using Indiana limestone on the exterior, Italian marble in the interior, and Russian mahogany all throughout the house. The home itself has thirty rooms, including the ten bedrooms I mentioned earlier."

"Who needs that many rooms?" an older man exclaimed.

"Well," Megan said, "as a very important man, Mr. Whitley needs to demonstrate to his visitors that his home is equally important. So, in addition to the bedrooms, there are twelve bathrooms, a ballroom, three drawing rooms, a parlor, conservatory, billiards room, and Mr. Whitley's private office, as well as the outdoor amenities, including the tennis courts and a swimming pool, which has been drained for the winter.

"The property itself is ten acres, half of which is covered by a forest of red spruce and Eastern white pine, and it has its own lake and boating pavilion."

The older man whistled. "Pretty nice digs."

"They are at that," Megan said with a nod. "Mr. Whitley wanted to give his fiancée something special, and we feel that he has. You'll meet both Mr. Whitley and Eliza Moran later. Now, follow me."

She turned and walked in a measured pace down the corridor, and gestured to the paintings.

"Mr. Whitley employs a gentleman full time to constantly circulate between the auction houses of

London, Paris, Rome, and Berlin in order to purchase items for his home, including these paintings by the old masters." Her favorite picture by far was one of a woman reading in a window seat, illuminated by a shaft of sunlight. It was pretty much Megan's idea of paradise. "You'll also note the display cases filled with objects purchased during Mr. Whitley's own trips to Europe."

The visitors made sounds of appreciation as they passed cabinets filled with china, crystal, and gilded metal.

"Looks like a lot of dusting," a woman in a Christmas sweater said.

"This house employs ten housemaids who work under me, and our days are filled with a never-ending mountain of cleaning—every room, all the laundry, and the bathrooms. It doesn't stop!"

She chuckled ruefully.

"We also have Mr. Fredericks, the butler, as well as five footmen, a cook, three scullery maids, three kitchen maids, fifteen gardeners, and a chauffeur-slash-mechanic for Mr. Whitley's automobile."

"It's like a private army," the woman said in awe.

"It is! And it takes a considerable amount of work between myself and Mr. Fredericks to keep everyone in line."

Megan stepped inside an elegantly furnished parlor, its windows facing one of the snow-covered lawns. The room was trimmed in more vintage Christmas décor.

"Are we all here?" she asked, counting the number

of visitors. When she was sure that everyone in the tour group was present, she picked up a small enameled picture frame that sat atop a side table.

"This is a photograph of Mr. Whitley," she said.

The visitors pressed closer, all of them eager to get a glimpse of the mansion's owner.

"I wouldn't mind *him* in my Christmas stocking," one gray-haired woman said.

Megan glanced down at the picture. She'd looked at it hundreds of times, but still felt a little jump of excitement in her chest every time she did. At the time the photograph was taken, Charles Whitley had been in his prime. He was thirty-one, tall, with broad shoulders nicely filling out his custom-tailored suit jacket. Like many other men of his day, Charles Whitley sported a short, neatly trimmed beard. Standing behind his desk, he gazed at the camera with a single-minded intensity, as if trying to figure out not only how the camera worked, but how he could improve the process of taking photographs.

It was a striking image, and one she never tired of seeing.

"This was taken just before Mr. Whitley left for a trip to Paris in 1902."

"He looks kind of impatient," a woman with purple hair said.

"Standing still has never been something at which Mr. Whitley excels. You're all my friends, so I can confess something to you." Megan lowered her voice to an audible whisper. "I have a little crush on Mr.

Whitley. But never tell him! That has to stay between you and me."

The guests chuckled—even though Megan was telling the truth. She *did* have a crush on Charles Whitley. Most modern women nursed crushes on movie stars and rock musicians, but she was just a little in love with a man who had lived well over a hundred years ago.

No wonder her life seemed stuck.

"Your secret's safe with us," a woman said, smiling.

"Oh, thank you!" Megan pressed a hand to her heart. It was silly to pine for someone who had lived in another era, rather than focusing on finding someone special *now*. Well, she'd tried, but she hadn't been very successful at it—which was why, a month after she and Brandon had broken up, she hadn't gone out on a single date with anyone.

"When did Mr. Whitley die?" the older man asked.

Megan didn't have to feign her sadness. "He disappeared mysteriously in 1902, right after he returned from Paris. His disappearance was just a week before Christmas, as a matter of fact. No one has ever solved the puzzle of where he went, or why."

The visitors murmured with curiosity among themselves.

"Now," Megan said, "please follow me into Mr. Whitley's private study."

She took the guests through a large, heavy wooden door into another room. It was lined with shelves that were crammed full of books, and the furniture was substantial and masculine. The fireplace was lit, and two chairs flanked the stone, as if anticipating Charles Whitley to come in and sit down to read the newspaper.

Windows lined one wall, with the thick green velvet drapes pulled back to let in bright light from the snowy afternoon. Directly in front of the windows was the same desk that was in the photograph of Charles Whitley.

"This is my favorite room in the house." Megan stood beside the desk. "Mr. Whitley's study is the room where he spends most of his time. This desk is from the First International Exposition of Modern Decorative Arts held in Turin, Italy, in May of 1902. It's carved in the Art Nouveau style, which is extremely modern, and topped with red leather from Morocco."

"Sure beats working at my kitchen table!" the purple-haired woman said.

Megan smiled. "Mr. Whitley's work is extremely important to him, so he wanted to be sure that his desk reflected that. As you can see, he's in the middle of several projects."

She waved at the papers stacked neatly atop the desk. Lucite boxes covered the papers, ensuring that they couldn't be touched or decay from the atmosphere. Only under the supervision of one of the house's trustees could someone go through the papers covered with Charles Whitley's bold handwriting.

"This room is nearly identical to how Mr. Whitley left it right before his disappearance," she said. "Some papers were moved shortly after he disappeared, but we tried to keep the room as he would have left it."

"Kind of a neat freak, huh?" the boy with the mobile phone said.

"Mr. Whitley didn't become a self-made man by being sloppy," Megan answered. "So be sure to make your bed when your mom tells you to."

Everyone laughed, and Megan felt that familiar sense of peace and happiness that always came over her when leading tours. There was nothing better than making the past accessible to the present.

Being a tour guide didn't quite fulfill her need to share history with others, since it was limited to the visitors that came to the house. If only she could shape a generation's minds, and bring history alive for people evolving from teenagers to adults...*then* she'd feel she was fulfilling her true purpose. Being a history professor at the university would be a dream come true. Making that happen, though, was proving much more difficult than she'd expected.

But she was here now, teaching the visitors about history, and that nearly satisfied her need to educate others.

She continued, "It was a condition in Mr. Whitley's will that whomever inherited the house upon his demise was to preserve at least fifty percent of the home in its original condition—no changes could be made, so that future generations could learn from him. Which is precisely what was done."

She pointed to a beautiful gold and enamel clock

sitting on the desk. It boasted a large dial adorned with flowers, and a marble base capped with gilt fittings. The visitors murmured with appreciation.

"Mr. Whitley brought this clock back from a trip to France, shortly before his disappearance. We don't know much about it, since it was purchased second-hand in 1902. Our guess is that it's an eighteenth-century mantel clock, perhaps from one of the expert clockmakers in Switzerland."

"All the other clocks in the house are working," the little girl with the thick curls said, "but this one doesn't."

Megan shook her head. "No matter what our engineers and experts do, they can't seem to make the clock work. We've studied Mr. Whitley's journals for an answer, to no avail. All of Mr. Whitley's journals are housed in our archives here in the mansion. Go ahead and have a look around the study, but be sure not to touch. We have many rare books in here, including first editions of Charles Dickens's *Bleak House*, and Jane Austen's *Sense and Sensibility*."

The guests drifted around the room, commenting on the many books it housed. It was a book lover's dream room, and so Megan adored it. Her own personal library, which was admittedly extensive, consisted mostly of battered history books found in used bookshops, as well as well-worn paperback romances.

The visitors also looked over the desk that had been so perfectly preserved. It was indeed a monument to industry, and had been wildly expensive back in its own day. Today, the desk was priceless.

The little girl took particular interest in the papers, bending close to study them, which made Megan smile.

After a few moments, Megan said, "I'll show you the rest of the house, including Mr. Whitley's conservatory, his bedroom, and Eliza Moran's bedroom. She inherited the house after Mr. Whitley's disappearance, and eventually married and raised a family here. Not only will you meet Eliza Moran and Mr. Fredericks, the butler, you'll also meet Mr. Whitley himself!"

The crowd made quiet sounds of anticipation.

"On our way, be sure to take a good look at the Christmas decorations—we're using genuine turn-of-the-century décor, including glass ornaments from Lauscha, Germany, and pine boughs taken from this property's forest."

As the visitors filed out of the study, she said, "And don't forget: in six days, it will be Christmas Eve, and the mansion will host a big holiday party for everyone. Back in his time, Mr. Whitley used to throw a Christmas party for his employees at the old Belham Hotel. The steel mill still holds its party at the hotel, but we have our own festive gathering for visitors and the local community here at the mansion."

"Sounds wonderful," a woman said.

"It is! Be sure to bring your friends and family." Everyone who worked at the Whitley-Moran Mansion loved hosting the party, and it attracted people from nearby areas. Some visitors even came from New York City and Montreal to be part of the holiday fun. "Please go ahead to the next room on your left."

More visitors left the study, and Megan placed a hand on the little girl's shoulder. The girl paused.

Megan waited until everyone had gone before bending down to the girl.

"Thanks for being my shill, Sophia," she whispered.

The girl beamed. "Sure! It's not just because my dad works here. Charles Whitley's my hero. Someday, I'm going to be an inventor and entrepreneur, just like him."

"I'm looking forward to seeing what you invent. Now catch up with the other guests, so nobody suspects we're in cahoots."

Sophia nodded, and hurried on.

The rest of the tour went smoothly, with visitors asking questions and admiring not just the house itself, but its festive decorations. In the preserved kitchen, they met Mr. Fredericks, played by Dan Romano, who showed them the china collection and wine cellar, and talked about what was required to house and feed a staff the size of the mansion's.

Upstairs, by the bedrooms, the guests were introduced to Charles Whitley's fiancée, Eliza, who was played by Amber Parisis. She discussed what it was like to be a hostess for some of the biggest society events in her day, and gave them a brief tour of her impressive closet that was the size of most people's living rooms.

The highlight of the tour came when the guests went into the ballroom and met Charles Whitley himself, who was enacted—with some self-importance—by Ryan McConnell.

While Megan liked Dan and Amber, she wasn't so crazy about Ryan. He never hung out in the break room or joined after-hours gatherings, insisting that the real Charles Whitley would never have gotten friendly with the staff. It rubbed Megan the wrong way, so she tried not to be around Ryan very much.

The guests were encouraged to ask Mr. Whitley questions, and while Ryan certainly didn't have the technical knowledge or imagination of Charles Whitley himself, he'd studied enough about the man to be able to reasonably field inquiries about how he'd amassed such a substantial fortune within just a few years, and what innovations he was most proud of.

Inevitably, someone asked about Whitley's disappearance, and Ryan always said that he'd gone on an adventure—which was a nice way to say that nobody knew what had happened to Charles Whitley.

It was a little spooky to consider him vanishing, and they played this aspect up during tours around Halloween. But for Christmas, they focused on the big party and keeping everything festive.

After the guests met Mr. Whitley, Megan escorted them to the front door.

"Don't forget about our holiday party on Christmas Eve!" She waved goodbye to the departing visitors.

Smiling to herself, she closed the door and leaned against it.

A warm, pleased glow settled through her. She never finished a tour without feeling satisfied. She, and the rest of the cast, had encouraged a love of history in the visitors, which was exactly the point of turning the mansion into a museum.

She checked the watch she kept pinned on the inside of her sleeve. There was still an evening tour in a couple of hours, which meant she had a bit of time to get off her feet and read a few pages of her latest book—a historical romance set in the Victorian era where the heroine was an artist and the hero was a gentleman returning from war.

Her smile faded when she remembered what Brandon used to say about her love of history and historical romance. *You're stuck in the past. I want someone who's with me now.*

Megan shook her head as she walked toward the staff break room. She wouldn't be gloomy, not when Christmas was so close.

The break room had once been the servants' dining hall, back when the mansion had a staff. It had been modernized with a kitchenette and a nice set of cubbies for the employees' possessions. Instead of one long table, smaller round tables were dotted around the room, and potted poinsettias were placed on each table to add to the house's holiday atmosphere. High windows let in dazzling December afternoon light.

"Nice work today, Dan." Megan poured herself

A Timeless Christmas

a cup of coffee in her favorite reindeer mug and sat down next to Dan and his daughter, the girl with the curls. "And thanks again for the help, Sophia."

Sophia looked up from drawing yet another idea for an invention. "You bet! I expect full payment with a hot cocoa at Tina's Diner."

Megan chuckled and looked at Dan, who was still wearing his butler's uniform.

He raised his hands. "I can't help it if my daughter has good negotiating skills."

"That's what comes from idolizing a business genius," Megan said. "Got to be ruthless to get ahead."

"Speaking of getting ahead," Dan said, "have you gotten that letter of recommendation from Professor Coyle yet?"

Megan fought a grimace. "Not so far. She hasn't responded to my emails."

Dan fixed her with a parental look. "You've got to be more assertive if you want that letter, Megan. I know how much you want that teaching position at the university, and academic jobs don't just fall into your lap, even if you do have a PhD in history."

"I know. You're right." She sighed. "I just worry that I'm being pushy. Besides," she added, "I'm really busy leading tours and getting ready for the Christmas party here."

Dan didn't look convinced, but before he could speak, Sophia said, "Daddy! Stop being so much of a dad."

Both Megan and Dan laughed.

"Okay, okay, you got me," he said. "I'll make it up to you. Join Sophia and Lydia and me for dinner. You can even bring Brandon."

Megan's smile faded. "Brandon is in the past tense."

A slightly awkward silence fell.

"Good," Sophia declared.

"Sophia Grace!" Dan said in admonishment.

His daughter jutted out her chin. "He was mean and thought history was boring."

"Well," Megan said sadly, "he thought I was a boring girlfriend, too."

"I don't like him," the little girl said.

"Me neither," her father added.

Megan rose, and she tapped a finger on Sophia's nose. "Thanks, guys. I'll be okay. It's been almost a month, and while I don't miss him, the breakup still hurts." As she went to the sink to rinse out her cup, she joked, "That's what happens when you compare every guy you meet to Charles Whitley. Nobody stacks up."

"Try being almost married to him." Wearing her Eliza costume, Amber came into the staff room and walked to the small fridge. "Visitors can't get over the fact that Eliza married Whitley's business rival. They look at me like I'm some kind of monster."

"It certainly is a detail that catches their imaginations," Megan said. "You have to wonder what Eliza was thinking."

"I do wonder." Amber grabbed a container of salad from the refrigerator and popped it open. "But then,

I like the process of getting into character and finding out someone's hidden motivations." She shrugged. "It's the actor in me."

"There are still performances of the holiday one-acts, right?" Dan asked. "We wanted to take Sophia."

"We're performing every night this week except Christmas Eve and Christmas Day." Amber took a bite of her salad.

"I'll definitely check it out," Megan said. "I bet you steal the show."

Before Amber could answer, Ryan, dressed in his Charles Whitley costume, stormed into the break room. Hot on his heels was Phillip Tran, the museum's manager.

"Be reasonable, Ryan," Phillip pleaded.

"I will not!" Ryan struck a pose, his arms crossed over his chest. "It's time for you to give me the recognition I deserve."

Amber, Megan, and Dan exchanged worried looks. This wasn't good.

"The Christmas party's just six days away," Phillip said. "Everybody looks forward to the speech given by Charles Whitley."

"Which means that *I* am the star of the museum." Ryan lifted his chin. "And if that's true, my salary should reflect that. I've asked for a raise before, and you hedged. Now I'm *demanding* what I'm worth."

Phillip's brow furrowed. "There's just not enough money in the budget to give you the raise you want."

Megan watched this exchange with concern. She

and her fellow reenactors were given a decent but not excessive salary, with the rest of the money from ticket sales, grants, and donations going to the upkeep of the mansion and other expenses.

"Come on, Ryan," she said. "We're all working here because we love history, not because we want a plush lifestyle."

"I don't know about *you*," Ryan said, and sniffed, "but *I* have ambition. And if this establishment can't give me the money I deserve…" He glared around the room. "…then I quit."

A shocked silence fell. Megan stared at Ryan, hardly believing what he'd just said.

"We have an evening tour coming through in an hour," Phillip said in a stunned voice.

"And the Christmas party in six days," Megan added.

"You should've thought of that before refusing to meet my demands." Ryan untied his cravat, pulled off his turn-of-the-century jacket, and shucked his embroidered waistcoat before throwing all of them onto the floor. "Merry Christmas!"

With that, he marched from the room.

Megan's heart sank. Without Charles Whitley, there was no tour, no party…no anything. He was the museum's biggest draw, as evidenced by their visitors' posts on the museum's social media accounts. Maybe the museum could try to get by without someone playing Charles Whitley—saying that he'd disappeared—but their attendance numbers would drop precipitously.

Suddenly, Dan jumped up and grabbed the clothing from the floor. "I'll do it. I'll play Whitley."

Sophia gasped with excitement. "Yes! Daddy, you've wanted to be Mr. Whitley for forever!"

That was the first Megan had ever heard of Dan's ambition, and his cheeks reddened a little at being called out by his daughter, but he looked at Phillip. "Well?"

"You don't have a beard," Phillip said.

"I can get one from the university's theater department."

"He'll make a great Charles Whitley," Megan said encouragingly.

"Give him a try," Amber added.

After a moment's deliberation, Phillip nodded. "Okay. Go get a beard and be back here in forty-five minutes." He hurried from the room.

"High five, Charles Whitley." Megan lifted her hand, and a grinning Dan slapped his palm against hers. "Go suit up."

"Ready to go?" Dan asked his daughter.

"Wait until Mommy hears about this! Let's get you in costume, Daddy!" Taking Sophia's hand in his, Dan quickly left.

"Crisis averted," Amber said and exhaled in relief. "I love this job, and I need it, too. It's not as though community theater pays extravagantly."

"Now we all get to keep our jobs," Megan said.

As Amber finished her salad, standing over the sink, Megan sank down onto a chair. She was glad for Dan, and felt the same relief that Amber felt.

They'd come much too close to missing out on the holiday. Even if Megan couldn't have everything she wanted—like that teaching job, or someone special in her life who accepted her as she was—there was always Christmas.

CHAPTER TWO

Meanwhile, in 1902...

"Be sure to put my trunks in my room," Charles Whitley said to the two footmen as they stood in the foyer. "And take these crates into my study. Carefully. They're my purchases from Paris, including something I intend to give Eliza."

He pointed to the large wooden boxes marked FRAGILE.

"Yes, Mr. Whitley," one of the footmen said.

"And bring a crowbar."

"Yes, sir."

It felt good to be back home again after so long an absence. Charles had been living in hotel rooms for the past few weeks, and while the rooms had been luxurious, there was something so right about sleeping in his own bed, beneath the roof of the house he'd designed and built.

Besides, his home was certainly the elegant equal

of any of the stylish, sumptuous hotels of Europe. He'd worked very hard to ensure that everyone who entered his home knew that he was worthy of their respect. From almost nothing, he'd built a massive steel empire—to the cost of nearly everything else in his life. Work always came first.

"Is that a Christmas gift?" Rosie asked as she came into the foyer. As usual, the housekeeper wore her apron perfectly starched and her cap neatly in place. Charles wouldn't rely on her if she'd been in any way slovenly. He needed her to keep his own tumultuous life in order.

He shot Rosie a questioning glance.

"Because Christmas is in less than a week," Rosie explained. "I assumed you intended to give your fiancée a gift for the holiday."

"If it will make her happy to say it's a Christmas gift, then we'll call it that."

His housekeeper rolled her eyes. It was a measure of how much Charles relied on her that he was willing to endure her impertinence.

"My goodness," she said. "For someone who throws his employees such a lavish Christmas party each year, you truly have the least appreciation for the holiday."

After pulling a journal from his valise, Charles strode from the foyer and headed toward his office, knowing that Rosie would follow him. He walked beneath the coved ceilings and past the cabinets he'd paid to have stocked with beautiful objects from around the world—though he never stopped to look at his purchases. Always, he was too busy to meander and take his time. Slowing down was for those who didn't have a destination.

As he had anticipated, Rosie was fast on his heels as he walked.

"The date on the calendar is entirely arbitrary," he said over his shoulder, "and should have nothing to do with how we lead our lives. However, my employees enjoy the holiday, and I'm not an unfeeling monster."

He stepped into his study, barely seeing the custom-bound books and rare volumes. Instead, he went quickly to his desk, where he set down his journal. Tidy stacks of papers awaited him, and he was gratified to see that they had been undisturbed during his month-long working visit to France. Rosie ensured that the rest of the staff did not touch any of his papers or documents, not even to clean. Consequently, a thin layer of dust had settled over everything on his desk.

"Glad to hear it," Rosie said tartly, standing in front of his desk. "Even if you don't actually go to the party."

"Why should I? The hotel provides plenty of food and drink and other festive things. My employees don't need me glowering at everyone to make the night complete."

Two burly footmen brought one of the crates into his study, with a crowbar balanced atop the wood. When they set it down on the imported Persian rug, Charles grabbed the crowbar.

The tool felt good in his hands. He'd grown rich

using not just his mind but his hands, and it never hurt to get back to the skills that had first propelled him from poverty into wealth. One never knew when fortune would reverse itself, and he'd find himself with nothing again.

Using the crowbar, Charles pried the lid off the crate. It made a satisfying crack. He set both the tool and the lid aside and carefully extracted the crate's contents.

"Oh, that's lovely," Rosie said.

It was a gold-plated mantel clock with an intricate enameled design on its case and pieces of white marble for its base. Charles couldn't guess at its age, despite his research into the topic, though it seemed at least a hundred years old. There was no maker's mark, either.

He did know that he had to bring it back from Paris to give to Eliza. She'd been rather glum over his long trip abroad, despite his explanation that he had needed to travel to visit French steel mills.

You're either at your desk or at your mills, she'd often say to him. *But hardly anywhere else. You're almost never with me.*

I'm here now, he would answer.

She'd place a hand on his heart. *Not here, you aren't.*

Poor Eliza. She'd been raised in a life of privilege, and while her father was one of the preeminent men in shipping, Mr. Haas delegated his responsibilities—far more than Charles ever did. Eliza wasn't used to the long hours or prolonged absences that were necessary to keep a vast business empire thriving. But after accepting Charles's offer of marriage, she'd quickly learned that theirs was to be a relationship that would have to endure frequent separations.

He liked Eliza, and he felt reasonably confident that she liked him as well. Theirs would be a marriage based on mutual respect. A young woman from her social background was expected to make an advantageous match, and marrying her would not only ensure her material comfort, but his place in New York's upper ranks. They both benefitted from the union.

This clock seemed like a good way to make up for the fact that he hadn't been around for nearly a month. She liked pretty things, and the clock was quite handsome.

Perhaps he wasn't exactly a doting fiancé, yet he fully intended to give his future wife every material comfort.

"I bought it at the *Marché aux Puces de Clignancourt*." He set the clock on his desk and stood back to study it.

"Sorry to inform you of this, Mr. Whitley," Rosie said, "but it doesn't seem to work."

"And I fully intend to get it running again before I give it to Eliza." It presented a puzzle, and he did enjoy solving puzzles.

"By the by, she sent you a letter. It was delivered yesterday." The housekeeper pointed to an envelope on his desk.

"Why didn't she send a telegram?"

"Maybe she's not as in love with technology as you

are." Rosie cleared her throat and looked at the letter meaningfully.

"All right, I'll read it now." Charles picked up the envelope and cut it open with an ebony-handled letter opener. He pulled out several sheets of pale yellow paper and scanned Eliza's delicate script.

"What does it say?"

Charles glanced at her. "I wonder why I tolerate your cheek."

"Because without me, you'd spin in circles like a top. So, what's in the letter?"

He skipped over Eliza's professions of love and her impatience for their wedding, which was scheduled for the spring, the earliest his schedule could possibly permit it. Eliza wanted a honeymoon, and the thought of spending at least two weeks away from his work nearly gave him apoplexy. Still, he'd secured them a trip to a number of the capitals of Europe, staying in the most exclusive hotels. That would certainly make the Society pages of the newspapers.

However, given that the current state of his nuptials was his and his fiancée's business, he decided to tell Rosie only the other part of Eliza's letter.

"She has invited me to her parents' Manhattan home to celebrate the holiday," he said.

"Very good." Rosie headed toward the door of the study. "I'll tell Mr. Abernathy to pack you for the trip. You'll need something for Christmas Eve, of course, and Christmas morning, and—"

"I'm not going."

The housekeeper stopped short and spun around. "You're not? But...it's Christmas."

"Whether or not it's the twenty-fifth of December is unimportant to me. I've worked on Christmas since I was fourteen, and I'm not going to stop now." He pulled a few sheets of paper out of the top drawer of his desk. "While I was abroad, I had some marvelous new ideas for improving the production line. Between that and fixing Eliza's clock, I'm simply too busy to take time off for the holiday."

"Mr. Whitley—"

Gaining steam, Charles said, "And do you think Harold Moran doesn't work on Christmas? I'm sure he's just waiting for me to step away from my responsibilities so he can swoop in and have his business overtake mine." The very thought made Charles's blood boil. Moran would *not* best him. Charles would make certain of that. "Absolutely not."

"Oh, but sir—"

Charles exhaled. "Thank you, Rosie. That will be all."

She must have seen that he would not be argued with, because she clamped her lips together and walked briskly from the room.

Alone—finally.

After making certain that no one else was nearby, Charles crouched down and carefully removed a piece of the floorboard. Beneath it was a twelve-inch-by-twelve-inch compartment, lined with green felt. He grabbed his journal from atop the desk.

Flipping through the pages, he reviewed the designs for new inventions he'd sketched while in France. After seeing some of the modern French processes for milling steel, he'd been struck with ideas about how to make his own product much faster, as well as stronger and more durable. The moment this tedious holiday season was over, he'd be in touch with the patent office.

Charles set the journal in the slot, then put the piece of floorboard back in place. He'd had the compartment installed during the house's construction. Perhaps some might view his extreme caution as overly guarded, but he'd spoken truly to Rosie. His rival, Harold Moran, was ruthless in his determination to make his empire more successful than Charles's. Only two months ago, Charles had been forced to fire a top-level manager when it had been revealed that the man had been feeding Moran secrets.

Moran had been Charles's constant source of irritation and anxiety for nearly a decade. It seemed as though they were perpetually stuck in a race with each other, both striving to be the first to reach the finish line that kept being pushed back farther and farther. Charles would have an idea, and mere days before he could file the patent, Moran would beat him with an idea that was almost identical—except Moran employed a research staff of half-a-dozen engineers while Charles developed ideas on his own.

Charles would skip sleep entirely in order to personally travel to a new iron ore mine to secure more materials to create steel, knowing that Moran would try to get there before him and buy up all the ore.

Charles had even caught Moran eyeing Eliza at various society functions, and *that* was unacceptable.

He pushed his desk back into place before planting his hands on his hips to survey the compartment's disguise.

In your eye, Moran.

Needing a moment to gather his thoughts, he turned and gazed out the window. The land surrounding his substantial home was also expansive. It never failed to strike a chord of gratification in him to think that these acres belonged to him, when just over fifteen years earlier, he'd barely been able to afford a straw-stuffed mattress in a boarding house room he'd shared with seven other boys. But this land and this house were *his*.

Yet as he searched for a feeling of being grounded, of belonging...nothing came. He was still the same rootless kid he'd been so long ago, struggling to find a place for himself but coming up empty-handed.

Needing to fix himself firmly in place, he looked at the moon.

He lifted a brow in surprise. The moon was a deep red. As he watched, the dark disk of the Earth's shadow slid across the moon.

A lunar eclipse. Not something that came around very often.

He'd make a note of it later in his private journal. For now, he had to finish reading the rest of Eliza's letter. Perhaps that would make him feel as though he belonged somewhere.

Picking up the paper, his gaze went to the last few lines.

I know you so well, Charles. I know that you probably will not join my family and me for the holiday, just as I know that you will spend that time working.

I pray that you can slow down, live in the now, and enjoy Christmas. It's a magical time, and one I hope you can come to appreciate.

Affectionately,

Eliza

He frowned.

Slow down? Live in the now?

The future was a much more exciting place to be.

He put the letter to one side and pulled the clock closer. After examining it for a few moments, trying to determine what could be causing its malfunction, he took a small leather case with delicate tools out from the top drawer of his desk.

Charles bent down to analyze the source of the problem. He suspected it was too tightly wound.

He picked up a thin screwdriver and used it to adjust a few of the clock's intricate pieces—a small modification here, a little tuning there. Working on the device brought a smile to his face. There was nothing more enjoyable than getting lost in a technological puzzle, figuring out the problems, making something better.

If only his relationships with other people—including Eliza—could be as simple, or as gratifying.

Don't think about that now. Fix what you can and worry about the rest some other time.

He looked up when the clock suddenly began to whirr while its pendulum started swinging back and forth.

"There it is," he said aloud in triumph. "Haven't lost my touch."

With a sudden *twang*, a tiny piece sprang free from the clock, startling him. The moment the piece shot from the device, the clock stopped working.

Blast.

He looked around the desk, searching for the missing piece. It was nowhere to be found. Perhaps it had fallen to the floor.

He crouched down, running his hands over the floorboards and thick carpets. "It's got to be around here somewhere."

But the more he searched, the less certain he was that he could ever find the piece.

With a frustrated exhale, he straightened.

He started in shock.

Christmas decorations were everywhere. They covered his study, from the tree covered with ornaments in the corner, to the swags of pungent evergreen hung around the room, and even the arrangement of red and green candles on the fireplace mantel.

"How…?"

Someone must have snuck in while he was on the floor and decorated his study. But he hadn't heard them, and the idea that even a team of silent workers could trim the room in Christmas decorations in the span of less than a minute was absurd. He knew what marvels technology could produce, and *this* was beyond the power of the best, most advanced steam engine.

Many footsteps sounded in the hallway. A moment later, nearly a dozen people in the strangest clothes he'd ever seen entered his study. For one thing, most of the women wore trousers, including very snug trousers fashioned of denim.

Leading the group of strangers was a pretty young woman in a housekeeper's uniform.

"Right this way, everyone," she said in a bright, musical voice. "Here's Mr. Whitley's study."

The woman was *not* Rosie. Charles had never seen her before, and he knew all the members of his staff. And he never gave anyone permission to bring strangers into his study.

"Excuse me," he said crossly. "What are you doing in my home? Did Rosie or Abernathy let you in?"

The woman in the uniform smiled, though there was a hint of confusion in her look. "*I'm* Rosie."

"See here," he said, coming around his desk, "whoever you people are, you're trespassing in my home, and I want you all to leave immediately or I will summon the constable."

As he spoke, many of the strangers in their peculiar outfits held up small, brightly-hued objects the size and shape of a deck of cards and, grinning, aimed them at him.

"Who are you?" a man asked him.

"I'm Charles Whitley—who are *you*?"

Instead of answering, the man just held up his little device and stared at the other side of it, his attention rapt.

The woman who called herself Rosie edged closer to him. With her so near, he could see the charming hazel hue of her eyes, and her cap partially covered her dark curls.

"Uh, hey," she said under her breath, "I thought Dan was playing Whitley."

"I beg your pardon!"

She looked over at the people invading his home and his study. "Whoever you are, you're doing a great job. Keep it up. They really think you're Charles Whitley."

"Because," he said hotly, with no attempt to speak in an undertone, "I *am* Charles Whitley. Now, if you would be so kind. Get. Out. Of. My. House."

CHAPTER THREE

I*'ve heard of method acting*, Megan thought, *but this guy is* really *committed to the role.*

The handsome stranger glared at her and the visitors. His posture was impeccable, and whoever made his costume had done amazing work. The custom coat of his sack suit fit his wide shoulders flawlessly, and the matching waistcoat hugged his torso. His tie was in a perfect four-in-hand knot and looked to be genuine silk. Even his two-toned ankle boots appeared handmade and exactly right for a man of 1902.

He was a perfect double for Charles Whitley, too. His dark hair was styled just like Whitley's, while his neatly trimmed beard looked identical to the photograph. Plus, he was flat-out gorgeous, with a strong jaw, high cheekbones, and vivid blue eyes beneath thick eyebrows.

But she had to keep pretending she was Rosie, and Rosie never stared at her employer with moonstruck eyes.

Glowering, the man went to the candlestick

telephone at the edge of the desk. Back in 1902, the phone had been the height of technology. Now, it was just a prop, not connected to any line. He picked it up, holding the receiver to his ear, and spoke into the mouthpiece.

"Operator! Operator! Get me the police!" He scowled, appearing angry that there was no voice on the other end of the line. "What the deuce?"

Wow—this guy was really good. But he was getting a little carried away with playing the part.

"All right, ladies and gentlemen." Smiling cheerfully to hide her bafflement, Megan stepped forward. It was probably a good idea to end the tour now, because this guy was messing up the order—Charles Whitley made his appearance at the end of the tour. "Let's move on to the gift shop, where you can find lovely souvenirs. It's just at the front of the house."

As the visitors filed out, they continued to use their phones to record "Charles Whitley."

The man in question pointed an accusing finger at the mobile phones. "What in gracious *are* those?"

The guests chuckled. Then they walked out, heading toward the gift shop.

Megan lingered rather than continuing on with the visitors. Whoever this guy was, he was doing an impressive job of playing Whitley.

"You're supposed to be in the ballroom," Megan said.

"Why? I'm not throwing a party."

Oh, boy, this person was deep in his character. Still, she had to give him credit.

"That was incredible," she said. "Even Ryan wasn't that into playing the part."

He scowled at her. "I have no earthly idea who or what you are talking about."

Dan appeared at the doorway to the study, dressed in the Whitley costume. He sported a decent-looking fake beard, but compared to the newcomer, he was far less impressive.

Coming into the study, Dan looked at the stranger in confusion. "I heard some guests saying that Charles Whitley was in the study, not the ballroom. What's going on?"

"I would like to know the same thing!" the unknown man said.

"He's dressed like Charles Whitley," Dan said to Megan. "Why's he dressed like Charles Whitley?"

"I keep telling everyone it's because I *am* Charles Whitley."

Dan frowned. "But *I'm* supposed to be Whitley."

"Maybe Phillip double-booked the part?" Megan suggested.

At that moment, Phillip hurried into the study. He stared at the stranger with admiration.

"Wow—I'd heard from the visitors in the gift shop that our Charles Whitley was incredible," Phillip said, "but *this* is spectacular." He pulled his phone from his pocket. "Our social media presence is blowing up."

40

"Social media…?" The stranger's expression grew more and more bewildered.

Phillip turned his phone around to show everyone the videos of "Charles Whitley" telling the visitors to his house to leave. Comments popped up at the bottom, saying things like, "LOL" and "OMG this guy is blowing my mind!"

"Didn't you hire him?" Dan exclaimed.

"No," Phillip said, "but I've been calling around town to let everyone know we're down an actor. Even with you playing Whitley, we needed a Fredericks." He looked at the newcomer with admiration. "I guess our new friend here heard the news and thought he'd make a better Charles Whitley than Fredericks."

"But—"

Phillip turned to the stranger. "If you want the job, it's yours. Sorry," he added to the scowling Dan, "but this guy is amazing."

Dan muttered something under his breath. He tore off his fake beard and stuffed it into his pocket.

Though Megan ached for him, knowing how much he wanted the role, when she glanced down at the image on Phillip's phone, her attention was riveted.

"We're going viral," she said in shock. "That video already has a thousand views in less than five minutes."

"Viral? As in, an illness?" The stranger stepped forward and snatched the phone from Phillip. He peered down at the screen. The expression on his face shifted from baffled to horrified. "Is that date correct? The year is accurate?"

"It should be," Phillip said. "Yesterday I updated the OS, so the glitch with the date was fixed."

The phone dropped from the stranger's hand. It landed with a soft thud on the carpet. He stared at Megan, his eyes wide with shock, his face pale.

"Are you okay?" she asked anxiously.

"I've read Wells's *The Time Machine*, and it seemed so unbelievable, but…I think it's real."

His gaze held hers, and the look of stunned amazement in his eyes made her heart contract. He seemed lost.

"As incredible as it sounds," he said in a wondering tone, "I've traveled a hundred and sixteen years into the future."

Dan, Phillip, and Megan all traded disbelieving looks.

Either the stranger was delusional, or deeply committed to method acting.

Or—crazy as it seemed—he really was from the past.

But that couldn't be. Could it?

Surely, Charles had to be dreaming. That had to be the only explanation for the outlandish world he found himself in.

Yet everything seemed very real. He could smell the evergreen boughs hanging from the walls. The glass ornaments hanging from the Christmas trees—one in *every* room—felt cool and delicate against his hands when he'd touched them.

And the sympathy in the gaze of the woman dressed like Rosie…it touched him deeply.

As he looked around what had been the staff's dining hall *one hundred and sixteen years ago*, he took in the new details of the room. In 1902, his house had been featured in numerous newspapers for its extensive use of electricity, but clearly that technology had progressed considerably, given the sheer number of lights that blazed from every corner and in the ceilings.

A metal box that hummed was positioned near the modern sink, and when Charles opened it, cold air rushed out.

"A home refrigeration unit powered by electricity?" he murmured to himself. "My goodness."

He pulled out a small, clear container that was far too lightweight to be glass. Perhaps it was a variety of polymer. A note had been affixed to the container, reading Megan. Tiny cakes made of rice, topped with what appeared to be pieces of raw fish, were inside the container.

"That's my sushi," the woman he now knew as Megan said, plucking the vessel from his hands. She put it back inside the refrigeration unit and shut the door.

"What is *sushi*?"

She looked at him with a perplexed frown. "Okay—you're still in character. It's a Japanese dish that rose in popularity in the United States during the 1960s. They sell it at restaurants and even in the supermarket."

Few of the words that came out of her mouth made any sense. Yet he distantly recognized that if he hadn't been so utterly confounded, he would have been pleased to talk with such an appealing woman. She seemed quite intelligent. And beautiful, as well.

Yet his mind spun too fast for him to fully appreciate her freckles and curls.

"Supermarket?"

She didn't answer him. Instead, she was pulled into a heated conversation between an Asian man and the gentleman who had been wearing a pantomime beard.

"You promised *me* the part of Whitley," the man wearing cheap, poorly constructed versions of Charles's clothing said.

"But the guests loved this guy, Dan," the Asian man replied.

"Maybe there's a compromise ," Megan said.

Charles looked down when someone tugged on the bottom of his jacket. A little girl with light brown skin and thick, curly hair stared up at him, her expression full of wonderment.

"I'm Sophia," the girl said. "Sophia Romano. It's nice to meet you."

Though Charles was in a fog of confusion, he could still summon his manners—the heavens knew he'd worked very hard to acquire the finer points of etiquette.

"Pleased to meet you, Miss Sophia. I'm—"

"Charles Whitley." Sophia nodded wisely. "I recognized you right away."

"You're not like the others who think I'm only *pretending* to be Whitley?"

The girl shook her head. "You're him."

A wave of thankfulness nearly overwhelmed him. It meant so much to simply be recognized for who he was—who he *truly* was. He nearly hugged the girl in gratitude.

Megan broke away from the other conversation to stand behind Sophia. She glanced between the girl and Charles.

"Your dad's pretty upset."

"He'll understand," Sophia declared. "Especially once he sees that this is the *real* Charles Whitley."

Megan chuckled, but then she quieted when she realized that the girl wasn't attempting to be humorous.

"That's impossible."

"I bet our phones seem impossible to him, too," Sophia said with the matter-of-fact tone of child explaining something to an ignorant adult, "but they're not. Who knows how time travel works?" She shrugged. "Maybe it's physics. Or maybe it's a Christmas miracle."

Charles wrinkled his nose at the mention of Christmas, but, given the elaborate way his home was decorated for the season, clearly the other people occupying his house had different opinions of the holiday.

He had more important things to consider right now, including *how* he'd traveled through time. And how he could get back to his own time.

"If you're going to work here," Megan said, holding out her hand, "I should introduce myself. I'm Megan Turner. I play the part of Rosie, the housekeeper."

"The woman who kept me in line." Charles couldn't stop himself from smiling at her. He shook her hand—she had a nice firm grip, but her skin was far too soft for a housekeeper—and she smiled back at him.

It was a delightful smile, spreading warmth through his chest.

"Charmed," he answered. "I am Charles Whitley."

She raised her eyebrows. "What's your real name?"

"That *is* his real name," Sophia said before Charles could.

"Right!" Megan said brightly. "It's method acting. I get it. Did you study at Yale? Maybe the Royal Academy of Dramatic Art or the Actors Studio? You should talk to Amber—our Eliza. She's an actor, too. She's in a show right now, so she's probably gone already so she can get to the theater in time."

Charles straightened. He might have risen up from the lower ranks of society, but he was certainly not so undignified as to ever pursue *acting* as a career.

"Miss Turner—"

"Hey there," the Asian man said, stepping nearer. He beamed at Charles and shook his hand. "I'm Phillip, the museum's manager. Can I just say how absolutely thrilled we'd be if you stayed on to play Whitley?"

"I…that is…"

Charles was supposed to enact the role of himself? How truly bizarre. Yet if he had to negotiate and navigate this new, futuristic world, staying close to home would be the wisest course. At least he knew his own house.

"This isn't fair," the man who had been pretending to be Charles said. "You said the part was mine."

"Five thousand views now, Dan!"

Charles had no idea what on earth that meant, but clearly, it was significant, because Dan deflated. Sophia quickly went to him and took his hand.

"Sorry, Daddy." She looked up at her father with sympathy. "I know what will cheer you up."

"What's that, butterfly?" Dan asked glumly.

"Mommy's waiting at home for us to decorate the Christmas tree!" She tugged him toward the door. "Come on."

Her father mustered a small smile.

"That definitely cheers me up." He went with Sophia, but not before throwing over his shoulder, "Charles Whitley would never have stolen someone's job. You're already wrong for the part."

Charles scowled, but Dan and Sophia disappeared, and there was nowhere to direct his anger.

"The gall of that man to suggest I'm behaving dishonorably!"

Phillip clapped his hands together. "Our last

tour is over, so we'll just see you back here tomorrow morning at eight. Do you need to brush up on the facts of Charles Whitley's life? We've got plenty of research materials."

"I think I'm familiar with what it means to be Charles Whitley," he answered drily.

"Great," Phillip said. "So...you'll start tomorrow. Sound good?"

Telling Phillip that Charles already had employment was an exercise in futility. It wasn't just that the man would never believe him—it was also the dawning realization that his job was no longer his at all. Surely Whitley Steel and Machines no longer existed. And what if it did? Some other man would run the place now. What did any of this mean?

His mind was a whirligig, making it impossible for him to make sense of anything. There was so much he couldn't comprehend. How had he gotten here? Could he go back? What if he couldn't? How would he survive?

Too many questions spun through his head, and he felt the ground beneath him shift as the world tilted on its axis.

"I need..."

He looked around. Megan had removed her cap and taken down her hair, which formed sweet waves over her shoulders. Her gentle face calmed him, but not fully. A man didn't just rocket through time without repercussions.

Only Sophia believed he was who he said he was.

If he insisted too vociferously, surely the others would think him mad, and madmen most likely were not allowed to roam the streets freely. The idea of being incarcerated or confined made his throat close.

"...I need to lie down."

He stalked from the room and headed toward his bedchamber. Megan and Phillip quickly followed.

The house, he was pleased to note, had barely changed. Everything looked exactly as he'd left it—with the exception of the Christmas decorations. Whoever lived in his home now had done an admirable job of preserving its appearance. The floors were polished, the lights blazed, and there wasn't a single cobweb to be found.

He climbed the stairs to the second story. It calmed him a little to see the paintings he'd acquired, reminding him of permanence and stability. His world might be falling apart, but at least the seventeenth-century paintings remained.

As Charles approached his bedchamber, Phillip said, "You can't actually sleep in this room."

"It's part of the museum," Megan added.

Charles drew up short. His way into his room was blocked by a burgundy velvet rope. Just beyond it lay his bed and all the familiar furnishings he had surrounded himself with, including a writing desk and leather chairs by the fire—but for some bizarre reason, he couldn't actually touch his own possessions.

"You've turned my home into a museum, as I specified in my will? And people actually come here?"

"Of course," Megan said. "Charles Whitley was one of America's most successful innovators. People love to hear about him and see how he lived."

It was difficult not to feel smug at this description of himself. However, that didn't change the fact that his home was not his anymore.

He had to concern himself with the basics before he could approach the larger questions and implications of time travel.

"If I can't sleep here, where *can* I go?"

Phillip sighed. "How about this—if you're so committed to playing the part, you can stay in the part of the house that's been modernized. People sometimes pay to use one or more of the rooms if they're renting the museum for a special event, like a wedding. Will that work?"

"I think so," Charles said after a moment. He was receiving permission to reside in the house he'd designed and paid for. How bizarre.

As if reading his mind, Megan asked, "Do you have any money?"

Charles patted his pockets. His heart sank.

"I seem to have left my billfold back in 1902." Unless the world had profoundly altered and people paid for goods and services with moon rocks, without any cash, Charles would find it very difficult to survive in the modern era.

"This is for your work today." Phillip pulled out his wallet and peeled off a few bills before handing them to Charles.

It was rather galling to think that he'd have to rely on anyone to provide his income. But he wasn't foolish enough to refuse it. He could ill afford to be too prideful when he was an outsider in a strange world.

"My gracious." He stared at the money in his hand. "Twenty dollars? Surely that's far too generous. I could rent a house for a month with this."

Megan stared at him, but Phillip only shook his head and laughed.

"You're too much, uh, 'Charles.'" Phillip did a strange thing with his fingers, forming them into brackets as he said Charles's name.

Charles opened his mouth to protest further, but Megan said quickly, "Phillip, I'll show Charles to his room. It's the guest room in the east wing, right? Why don't you head out and we'll see you tomorrow?"

Phillip looked a bit dubious, but after a moment, he nodded.

"Sure. Have a good night." Phillip gave a cheerful salute before trotting off.

When they were alone, Megan turned to him. "Come on. I think you'll be comfortable in the spare room."

"I should hope so," Charles said. "After all, I did have my home constructed with eight guest chambers—I might not be Vanderbilt, and this isn't Biltmore House, but my hospitality has not and cannot be faulted."

"Uh, right." Megan smiled uncertainly. "Follow me, and let's get you settled for the night."

CHAPTER FOUR

"Here it is," Megan said as she opened the door to the guest bedroom. "The family doesn't use the house anymore. Like Phillip said, these rooms are only used now if someone's renting the building and wants a space to relax, or stay overnight. Nothing's booked until the holidays are over, so you can probably stay here for as long as you want."

The man who insisted on calling himself Charles Whitley peered inside. "I don't recognize this room."

"A third of the house was modernized over the course of the last hundred years, so that's why it looks different."

Why am playing into his method acting?

He stepped into the room and immediately turned on a lamp on the bedside table. Then he switched it off, before turning it on again. "The entire house has been wired for electricity?"

Weird question. "Of course."

He walked quickly to the flat-screen television that

sat atop a dresser. "Is this some variety of generator? Or perhaps another piece of food storage equipment, like the one in the servants' dining room?"

"It's a TV. A television," she explained when he gave her a blank look.

"I remember hearing that word," he said with a thoughtful frown. "Constantin Perskyi talked of something called a *television* in his paper he read to the International Electricity Congress. But he was speaking of technology that was still being developed."

Megan's academic focus wasn't on the history of science, but she'd heard of the International Electricity Congress that had happened at the International World's Fair in Paris. In *1900*.

Clearly, "Charles" had done his homework. Maybe he was a history scholar in addition to being an actor?

"I'll show you." She picked up the nearby remote and turned the television on. It showed a couple holding hands as they walked on a sunny beach.

"Good gravy!" Charles cautiously approached the television and touched his fingers to the screen. "This is…some kind of viewing device?"

"Different stations broadcast different signals." She changed the channel, and a car appeared on the screen.

"Is that an automobile?" He stared at the screen. "It's moving so quickly. Surely its engine can't be more than thirty-five horsepower. That's what Wilhelm Maybach's Mercedes has."

A startled laugh burst from Megan. "Most cars

53

now come standard with at least a hundred-and-forty horsepower engines."

"My gracious!"

She smiled. "You're really into history, huh? I'm a history nerd, too."

"'Nerd?'" He tilted his head to one side.

"Um…" How could she define the word? "Someone who's extremely enthusiastic about a particular subject."

"Ah! Then I am most assuredly that." His smile was very cute, and made her stomach flutter.

The moment was broken when he pointed to the adjoining bathroom.

"Is that the water closet?"

Before she could answer, he pushed open the door and switched on the light. He marveled for a moment at the brightness of the room before staring at the toilet and bathtub. He flushed the toilet, then turned the tap on and made a sound of pleased surprise when the water flowed out.

"Plumbing has come a long way in a hundred and sixteen years." He fiddled with the knobs, and then yelped when the shower turned on, spraying the back of his head.

Megan clapped a hand over her mouth to keep from laughing.

"There should be some towels in there," she said, choking back a giggle.

"That is an excellent shower bath!" He came out of the bathroom, rubbing a towel over his damp hair. "It warms up so quickly. I would be most interested to see the water storage and how it's heated, if you would be so kind."

"Maybe tomorrow, we can ask Phillip to show you the changes that have been made to the house."

"Excellent. Thank you."

He was amazingly well-researched in the way he played the part. Even Ryan, who'd insisted that he was a great method actor, hadn't been so into the role.

Megan watched "Charles" as he continued to prowl around the room. Everything caught his interest, from the carpeting to the way the bed was assembled. The expression he wore was exactly like the one Charles Whitley had in the photograph she'd stared at so many times. It was the same look of focused curiosity that she'd found so captivating.

Either this Charles had also looked at that same photograph and was somehow incorporating it into his performance, or…

No. It couldn't be.

Still, this Charles had a genuinely delightful manner. He was the most respectful person she'd met in a long time. In fact, the only people she encountered who were so courteous were usually the older visitors to the house, as if learning proper etiquette was something from the distant past.

She was truly going bonkers if she was actually considering that *he* might be from the distant past.

Even so, being around him wasn't so bad. It was actually kind of nice.

"Hey," she said suddenly, "are you hungry?"

"In truth, I am." He tilted his head in thought. "I do believe that time travel stirs the appetite."

She chuckled. "How about I take you out to dinner?"

"While your generosity is appreciated," he said, straightening, "I am gentleman enough to insist on paying for your meal."

"Thanks," she said with a smile, "but I'm a modern woman who can buy her own dinner. Why don't we split the bill?"

He looked skeptical. "Everyone will think I'm a cad."

"Trust me, nobody is going to think that." She glanced down at herself and grimaced. "But I am going to change out of my Rosie costume before we head out. Did you bring some other clothes?"

"Unless my trunks came with me from 1902, I'm afraid this is all I have." He waved at his beautifully tailored suit.

Wow, he was definitely going the extra mile with his role playing. He must have heard about the opening at the museum and dropped everything so that he could play the part. Most likely, his wallet and possessions were back at his home, but he was too method to even acknowledge any of that.

But time travel certainly would explain his disappearance in 1902.

Oh my gosh—no way am I going to believe that. He's just an actor who's really good at playing the part.

"Okay, well, if anyone gives you a hard time about

it, we'll just say you work at the craft brewery. Those guys are always wearing vests and suspenders and taking selfies."

He looked completely confused by most of the words that left her mouth, but then he gave an adorable bow. "I await your pleasure."

"Looks like it snowed," Megan said excitedly as she and Charles walked from the house to her car. Her boots crunched in the snow, and the bare branches of the trees all wore white coats that sparkled in the evening.

After dark was always a special time at the mansion, with the large, rolling lawns disappearing into darkness and the black fringe of the treetops stretching up to the indigo sky. It helped that there was so much land around the house, so that there wasn't light pollution from other homes or buildings to diminish the feeling that one was truly back in another time.

She nestled deeper into her scarf, grateful for its protection from the cold. Charles didn't have a coat or a hat, though. If he really didn't have anything else to wear, she'd have to talk him into getting some warm, modern clothing. Commitment to a role was one thing—making himself ill by not dressing appropriately for the season was another.

"One thing's for certain," Charles said as his breath misted in front of him. "The weather hasn't changed."

"It still rains in springtime and snows at

Christmas, just like it's supposed to." Her car chirped as she activated her key fob, and the headlights flared brightly.

He stopped and gaped at the car.

"Did your automobile just turn itself on?"

"Wait until you see the dashboard." It was fun to pretend that he was some kind of time traveler rather than just a committed actor. Definitely, she ought to have him and Amber talk about what it took to create a convincing character. Amber was always searching out new ways to improve her acting craft, and Charles was unquestionably an amazing actor. She almost believed that he really was from the past. *Almost.*

After she got in, he opened his door then slid into the passenger's seat.

"Don't forget to fasten your seatbelt." She demonstrated how to secure it in place, and he quickly followed her instructions. "Get ready to go bananas. I mean," she corrected herself before he could ask about actual bananas, "prepare to be amazed."

She pressed the ignition button and the electronic dashboard blazed to life.

"This is…this is marvelous." He spoke on a whisper as he stared at the digital images. "An automobile that starts with the push of a button, and a galaxy of lights blazing right in front of you. I cannot believe that we have achieved such wonders in just over a century."

"Get this—my car is a hybrid. It runs on a combination of electricity and gasoline."

"No!"

"Yes!"

"A combustion engine that also employs electricity? How?"

She blinked. "I, um, don't know. But," she said with a bright smile, "I'll get back to you with more information. For now, let's eat."

It was a short ride from the mansion into town. There was a stretch of dark highway that had seen little development over the years, but as they neared Cutter Springs, more and more buildings popped up, all with their lights glowing in the dusk. She'd driven this route countless times, and could probably do it with her eyes closed, but her passenger stared out the window and made quiet exclamations of shock the whole time.

"Everything's so different," he murmured, watching the traffic as they got closer to the downtown square.

They passed the library and hospital, as well as the high school, and the theater where Amber was at that very moment likely getting ready to go on stage.

"There was one paved road in Cutter Springs," he said, "and one intersection. There was a single clapboard school and a general store. It surely was not this bustling metropolis."

She'd looked at old pictures of the town, and had seen photographs of the intersection—it didn't even have a traffic signal back at the turn of the century. Now, Cutter Springs was a thriving area that, while it hadn't lost its small-town charm, also boasted a university and a concert amphitheater where big-time musical acts would sometimes play during the summer.

Still, it was funny to hear Charles refer to Cutter Springs as a metropolis. Most everyone knew everybody else, and a walk to grab a cup of coffee from Donuts and Lattes often meant running into someone she knew from the fifth grade.

Don't you want to leave this dinky little town? Brandon had asked her.

It's not dinky, she'd said. *It's charming.*

Maybe to you, he'd retorted, *but just once I'd like to go to the hardware store without having to chat for fifteen minutes with the cashier.*

In Megan's opinion, that was one of the best parts about Cutter Springs. Everyone was a friend. But for some reason, Brandon had found it boring. Just like he'd found her boring.

Don't think about that now.

"We certainly didn't have so many Christmas decorations," Charles said grumpily.

Megan smiled as she caught sight of the tinsel garlands and electric stars that adorned the streetlights and traffic signals. The shops also sported cheerful wreaths, while their windows were festively painted with holiday greetings. The giant tree that would be used for the tree-lighting ceremony stood at attention in the town square, waiting to come to life with its colors blazing.

Strange that a man who threw a big Christmas

party for his employees sounded so grouchy about the holiday.

"Cutter Springs loves Christmas," she said, "and so do I. My brother and his wife are coming to town to spend the holidays with me and my parents. We can't imagine spending Christmas apart."

Charles nodded, then looked at a woman walking down the street. "I've observed that women wear trousers nowadays."

Megan looked at the woman whose skinny jeans were tucked into her fleece-lined boots. "They're comfortable. Warmer in this kind of weather, too."

To her surprise, he nodded. "Certainly they provide more freedom of movement. Bustles and petticoats were preposterous, not to mention impractical. Cycling costumes with their bloomers—*those* made sense." He pointed to a couple walking down the street, both of them on their phones. "Those little devices that everyone is obsessed with…?"

"Phones. And yes, we *are* obsessed with them."

"A telephone that you can carry in your pocket!" He exhaled. "Truly, a world of marvels."

As she waited for the light to change, she glanced at Charles out of the corner of her eye. He continued to look around with amazement, as if honestly seeing things like cell phones and women in jeans for the very first time.

Was he…not sane? Was *she* sane? She was actually considering the idea that the man beside her was really Charles Whitley. Certainly, he talked like a man from the beginning of the twentieth century, moved like one, and wore clothing that even an expert reenactor would envy. His knowledge of his time period, of Charles Whitley—it was exceptional. Only a very dedicated historian would know what he knew.

And the way he interacted with the world…

He couldn't be—could he?

Her brain shouted, *It's impossible!*

But her heart said, *Maybe…*

If it was true, if he *really* was Charles Whitley, then she was sitting beside the man who had revolutionized modern industry. More than that, through her research into Whitley's life, she'd learned about how hard he had worked to make his way in the world, the obstacles he'd overcome to rise in society, and his driven ambition. Had he not disappeared, he could've been even more famous than Ford or Edison.

Megan had also read Whitley's letters to and from his fiancée, and a picture had emerged for her of a man determined to succeed in business at the cost of his personal relationships. He had been Eliza's intended in name, but not in heart, always away from her or buried in meetings until the small hours of the morning.

That had made Megan sorry for both of them. Surely everyone needed love in their lives.

Goodness knew she could use some in hers.

A horn beeped and Megan snapped to attention. She put her foot on the gas and sent Charles an apologetic smile. "Daydreaming."

"I have been known to do a spot of woolgathering,

too." The corners of his eyes crinkled, and warmth stole through her.

He's not Charles Whitley. He just isn't.

But what if he is?

She pulled into a parking spot outside Tina's Diner. "Phillip's sister owns this place. You're going to love her food."

"The last time I ate was over a hundred years ago, so I've developed a bit of an appetite." Charles rubbed his hands together.

They went inside, though he looked a little surprised when she opened the door before he could do it for her.

"There's a song, 'Sisters Are Doin' It for Themselves,'" she said wryly as she held the door for him. "You ought to give it a listen."

"I've always believed that the notion that women were the weaker sex was utter balderdash," he said, walking through the door.

"And yet your company's board of directors had not a single woman."

"But I *do* employ women as supervisors at my mills and in my accounting department. So you see, I do believe in equality."

She tilted her head. "Touché." She waved toward one of the booths. "Let's have ourselves a very equal dinner."

As they sat, she looked around the restaurant. She'd eaten here countless times, but she now tried to look at it through Charles's eyes. People sat at the long counter, some on phones, some reading books or the newspaper, and one woman chatting with a waitress. Most of the booths were full of families grabbing a bite before continuing their Christmas shopping, if the packages heaped beside them were any indicator. Holiday music played, and Tina had put up a tree that had a mix of Western and Asian decorations as a nod to the diversity of Cutter Springs.

"I'll be right with you," Tina said to Megan as she took another table's order.

Megan didn't miss the way Tina's gaze lingered on Charles. And she wasn't the only one looking.

Oblivious to the fact that he was being scrutinized, he gazed with amazement at the electronic tablet that Tina used to take the orders.

"Honestly," he said, "I haven't been this impressed since my parents and I visited the Columbian Exposition in '93. We saw Tesla's induction motor, the electrified Egyptian Temple, and Elisha Gray's telautograph. They all promised a magnificent future, but this is beyond anything they imagined."

"That must have been amazing," she said.

"It was." His expression darkened. "My parents passed away just two months later."

Something occurred to Megan. "The museum keeps access to Charles Whitley's journals tightly restricted in order to preserve them and keep them from decaying from too much handling. Only people who have read those journals are aware that he went to the Exposition. I know all of those people—and you're not one of them."

"Because," he said with calm patience, "I wrote those journals."

All she could do was stare at him.

Is it…is it true?

"Hi, Megan!" Tina approached their booth, holding her electronic tablet. She sported a pair of reindeer antlers and a light-up necklace that looked like old-fashioned Christmas lights. She glanced at Charles. "This is the guy Phillip hired today?"

Megan shook her head to get back to reality.

"Tina, this is Charles."

"Wow, you really dressed the part." Tina stuck out her hand.

After a brief hesitation, Charles shook it.

"It's an honor to meet you. Your brother was extremely kind to me today. I won't forget that."

"Phillip's nuts about that museum," Tina said. "If he thinks someone can help support it, he wants them on board."

"Megan tells me your food is excellent, and I'm certain she spoke the truth."

Tina blushed. "Just a little home cooking."

"I hope you don't mind if I ask you to choose my meal," he said. "You *are* the expert."

"Oh, I like him," Tina said to Megan with a wink. "The usual for you?"

"Please." It was all Megan could do to speak one coherent word as she struggled to accept that the impossible *was* possible.

Tina punched their orders into her tablet and smiled before heading to another table.

When she'd moved on, Charles turned his attention back to Megan, who stared openly at him.

She couldn't help it. Everything about him shouted *Charles Whitley*. The things he knew weren't accessible to any outside a select few. And she couldn't deny that his manner, his conversation, all aligned perfectly with the man she liked to think she understood better than nearly anyone else. Despite the fact that Charles Whitley had been an extremely ambitious, determined man, his private correspondence had revealed a kind heart that had known its own share of hardship and loss. He'd passed that kindness on to others.

What she'd seen of the gentleness he'd shown to everyone he had encountered—okay, with the exception of threatening to have the tour group arrested—was truly extraordinary. Most modern people were too busy and self-involved to be so courteous.

Megan should have known that Brandon wasn't the guy for her when he'd been rude to the barista on their first date.

Not Charles. He had nothing to gain by being so considerate, and yet he was. As though treating people with dignity and respect was part of the fabric of his being.

"You seem to know an awful lot about me," he said, his gaze direct. "But now I think it's time I turned the tables. Tell me about yourself, Megan Turner."

CHAPTER FIVE

"What do you want to know?" Megan asked.

Charles considered the young woman sitting across from him. He wasn't sure she believed that he was, in fact, himself. However, she'd been quite caring and generous with her time. She was patient and explained things to him—most everything, anyway, since he was salivating over the idea of an automobile that ran on petroleum and electricity.

He also liked the sparkle in her hazel eyes and the wide, heartfelt smile that came so easily to her lips.

Guilt stabbed him. Within the past hour, he'd barely considered Eliza. She merited more than an afterthought, and he wanted to tell her so. He'd send her a telegram. Better yet, he would telephone.

I can't.

If he truly had traveled into the future—and everything seemed to indicate that he had—she'd likely passed away some time ago. Sadness descended at the thought, weighing him down. They hadn't had much time together, hadn't shared the future he'd planned where they would settle into the fullness of middle age and onward into their golden years, growing old together and watching the world change around them.

Had she mourned him? Did she find someone else?

Hopefully, she had—and had enjoyed a good, full life.

But he was truly alone here in the twenty-first century. And the thing he needed right now as he navigated this strange modern era wasn't money, or a place to lay his head, or even a meal.

He needed a friend.

Perhaps Megan could be that friend. He genuinely desired getting to know her better.

"You're employed at my house," he said, "as a guide, correct? You play the part of Rosie, my housekeeper."

He frowned. Rosie, too, was long gone. Surely she'd found worthwhile employment elsewhere, since she'd been so capable and competent. Hopefully, after years of service, she'd retired and found herself a snug little cottage where she could boss around a couple of cats.

"That's right." Megan nodded her thanks as Tina delivered two glasses full of water to the table. "I've been doing it for two years now while going to school."

"You're a student."

She flashed that smile. "Actually, as of September, I am now the proud owner of a shiny new PhD in American History."

He felt his brows rise in pleased surprise. "That

is truly impressive! I'm particularly glad to learn that people of both genders have access to advanced education. I'm afraid in my day, we weren't so equitable."

"There were women's colleges like Bryn Mawr and Vassar. Bryn Mawr actually was the first to offer graduate education all the way to the level of PhD."

"True, but places such as Bryn Mawr were not readily available to everyone."

She nodded thoughtfully. "You're right. There are some things about the past that I'm not as crazy about."

"A PhD in American History is no small achievement. I imagine you have big plans now that you've got your doctorate."

"Well," she said after a moment, "I'd really like to teach at our local university."

He slapped his palms against the table. "That's marvelous! When does your appointment begin?"

"I need to apply and be hired first." Her gaze slid to one side. "They require letters of recommendation, and I'm missing one."

"You should get it, at once."

"Oh, but…" She fidgeted with little paper packets that declared their contents to be SUGAR. "I'm just very busy with plans for Christmas, and there's so much to do at the house."

"Megan." He fixed her with a direct, but gentle, look. "Get that letter. Do you think I built my fortune by backing down from obstacles? I was fourteen when

I went to work at the steel mill, and I didn't let my bullying supervisor stop me from creating my first patent to improve the milling process."

"I hear what you're saying." Her mouth formed a tight line. "It's only…I don't have your strength."

He straightened, surprised by her answer. "You have earned a doctorate, which is no easy feat, and yet you doubt yourself. That's quite a contradiction." And a disturbing one, at that.

"As my dad would say, I'm a riddle inside a mystery, wrapped in bacon."

The silly analogy made Charles chuckle.

"It's funny," she said, her expression easing. "You're fascinated by the future, but I'm in love with the past. Especially your era."

"Does that mean that you believe me? That I'm truly Charles Whitley?"

For a long while, she said nothing. Anxiety climbed up his back, and he realized how important it was to have her accept that he had come from the past.

"You know," she said slowly, with a growing smile, "I think I do."

"You do?"

"Crazy as it sounds, I believe you really traveled here from 1902."

Charles's heart wanted to shoot out of his chest. He almost grabbed her hands and pressed a grateful kiss to them. Instead, he shut his eyes and exhaled with relief. He hadn't realized how crushing it had felt to have no one—except the girl, Sophia—believe him.

"Thank you," he said. "Knowing that makes me feel a little less alone."

"How did you do it? Travel through time, I mean."

He spread his hands. "I honestly have no idea."

At that moment, Tina returned with a tray bearing a large bowl of soup and a sandwich. She set the soup in front of Megan and the sandwich in front of him.

"A turkey sandwich with stuffing and cranberry sauce," Tina explained. "I've added a bit of lemongrass to the cranberry sauce. People love it, especially around Christmas. Enjoy."

When Tina had gone, Charles noticed that Megan had a soup spoon in one hand, and held a pair of long sticks in the other.

"These are chopsticks," she said. "People in Asia use them as utensils."

He had visited the Japanese pavilion at the Columbian Exposition, but didn't recall seeing anyone eating there. There had also been that Japanese food back at his house that Megan called *sushi*. Intriguing, how much more commonplace the food of other cultures had become in this era.

"How do you eat soup with them?"

She laughed, and lifted up her spoon. "That's what this is for. The chopsticks are for the noodles." She twirled them in her soup and lifted up a coil of long, thin, white strands. "This soup is a recipe from Vietnam. It's called *pho*."

"Vietnam?"

"Indochina. Want to try?" She held the chopsticks out toward him.

It wasn't easy balancing the chopsticks in his hands. He dropped them several times and could barely manage to dip them into the soup, much less coordinate them to grip the slippery noodles.

It took many attempts to swirl the noodles around the chopsticks and make them stay. They kept slipping back into the broth with a splash.

Guiding the noodles into his mouth also proved difficult, and once he did manage to secure them, he hesitated. How could he eat them without appearing utterly uncouth? Eating the noodles with a minimum of noise would prove to be a challenge, as well.

She chuckled. "It's okay—everyone slurps!"

With her permission, he slurped and finally got a bite of the noodles. A complex blend of spices filled his mouth.

"That's delicious."

"Tina says it's an old family recipe. Her grandma brought it with them when they emigrated in the '70s. The 1970s," she corrected herself.

Gracious, that was over forty years ago, but when he'd left his time, that had been seventy years in the future. He could barely keep up with the peculiarities that came with time travel.

He glanced around the restaurant, seeing people of every color.

"The world is much smaller now."

"You're right. You can be in Buffalo and talk to

someone in Hanoi via video calls—or you could get on an airplane and fly there in a day."

"My word." Energy sizzled through him as he considered the changes that had happened over the last hundred and sixteen years, and the literal world of possibilities that had opened up. "What a magnificent time to be alive."

She looked wonderingly at him.

"Wow, you're taking this whole time travel thing pretty well."

"As you said, I have always been fascinated by the future. For now, I get to live in it."

"For now?"

"This isn't my home," he said. "I need to think of a way to get back."

She nodded. "Of course you do."

"But in the meantime," he added, "I have a rather delightful guide."

Her cheeks turned an endearing pink. "I guess I'm really good at guiding people."

"No need to guess—it's true."

She blushed even deeper. "We should dig in before our food gets cold."

"You and Rosie have a lot in common." He picked up his sandwich. "She was always reminding me to eat, too."

"Smart woman," Megan said.

"The smartest."

The bill for their meal had been astronomically high, and he'd had a momentary panic as he contemplated paying it with his currently limited resources—until Megan had calmed him down by reminding him that Phillip would soon pay him for his work at the house. After they finished their food, Megan said there was one errand they needed to run before getting him essential supplies.

She drove them to a brightly lit shop. Astonishing. Businesses could be open so much later, thanks to the abundance of electrical lighting. From the glow inside the store, it could've been high noon, not seven o'clock in the evening.

"You can't exist in the twenty-first century without a phone," she said as they approached the shop.

"A telephone in your home was becoming commonplace in my time," he pointed out.

"Not a home phone. One that you carry with you, like mine." She held up the rectangular device.

He frowned. "Does that mean someone can reach you at any hour, in any place?"

"Most of the time."

"I'm not certain I would want that."

"If you really don't like a cellphone," she said agreeably, "you can turn it off, but it's a good idea to have one—just in case. Besides, it can be used for many things other than just phone calls. I'll show you later."

"I…" He forgot what he was going to say because they walked into the shop.

All around him were displays of dozens of the tiny devices. They were everywhere, and they all demanded his attention.

He walked up to one of them and picked it up. It fit into his palm and was surprisingly lightweight. Megan came over to him.

"I still can't believe this is a telephone," he said. "It's miniscule. And there are no wires."

"That's the future for you."

He turned in a slow circle, and read one of the numerous signs that hung around the shop.

"'Widest Network,' 'Unlimited Talk, Text, and Data.'" He shook his head. "None of this makes sense."

"It doesn't for a lot of people," Megan said with a laugh.

He studied the device, trying to figure out how it functioned. "My knowledge of mechanical and technological objects made me quite successful—wealthy, even—and yet this item that everyone carries now is an utter enigma." He knocked his knuckles against the shiny surface. "It's just a screen."

"Here." She poked something on the back of the mobile telephone, and a collection of tiny, colorful images appeared.

"And I can place a call to anywhere at any time, no operator necessary?"

"That's right." She nodded encouragingly. "As long as the battery's charged."

"Hi, folks, I'm Jaden!" A young black man with twists in his hair approached them. He wore a brightly-colored knit shirt with a logo stitched over his heart, and a tag with his name printed on it. "Can I interest you in an upgrade?"

"A *what* grade?" Charles's head began to throb. Normally, innovation excited him, but he felt the world rushing past at a speed too fast for him to keep up.

"Just something basic for a cellphone newbie," Megan said, thankfully stepping forward. "Do you have any flip phones?"

"Right this way," Jaden said.

The young man and Megan walked off. Charles hung back. Instead of joining them, he walked through the shop. It appeared that not only could one make telephone calls from these miniscule apparatuses, but they could function like miniature vitascopes, showing moving images—*in color*. It was difficult not to be transfixed by the images and he felt he could simply stare at them for hours. No wonder everyone nowadays walked with their heads down, staring at the items in their hands.

He turned one of the mobile telephones over. From his pocket, he drew out a diminutive screwdriver, something he always kept handy. Yet he couldn't find anything to unscrew. For a few moments, he fiddled with the device, trying to locate a means of opening it.

"Um, sir?" Jaden appeared, Megan beside him. "Can I help you with something? We prefer for customers to purchase a phone before they start tearing it apart."

Charles smiled sheepishly. It wasn't the first time

in his life that a shopkeeper had politely requested that he not disassemble the merchandise. Still, he exclaimed, "How the gravy does someone look inside one of these devices? I can't figure out how something works if I can't see inside it."

"We can do that later." Megan gently took the telephone from him and set it down on the counter. "I know it's a lot to take in, but we'll take it step by step, okay?"

Slowly, Charles nodded.

She held up a telephone that had actual buttons.

"I got you a flip phone, and I've put my number in it, so you can reach me whenever you need to. Maybe later, we can move you on to a smartphone, and I'll show you how to text, but for now, this should work just fine."

He didn't know what a *smartphone* was, and the only kind of text he was familiar with was between the covers of a book. Even so, his frown eased and the pressure that had been building in his head lessened. "You're exceptionally kind. And I *do* insist on paying you back."

"I know you will." She gave him a warm smile. "Just consider me your twenty-first-century tour guide. But now that we've got you settled with a phone, it's time to go shopping."

Charles tried not to look like he'd just fallen off the back of the turnip truck, but the giant building Megan called a "supermarket" astounded him. The ceilings were incredibly high, and from them hung extremely bright lights.

But even the amount of illumination was not nearly as impressive as the seemingly endless shelves laden with goods.

"We don't have a mega-mart in Cutter Springs," she said apologetically. "And the nearest one would be closed before we could get there, so a supermarket will have to do tonight."

He wasn't certain what a "mega-mart" might be, but if it surpassed a "supermarket" for size and variety of goods available for purchase, he would have likely suffered an apoplexy.

"There's so much to choose from," he said in amazement as Megan pushed a wheeled cart. He plucked a can from a shelf. "Tomatoes from Italy." He moved down the aisle and grabbed a crinkly, clear package from another shelf. "Noodles from Japan." Unable to contain his excitement, he rounded a corner and was presented with the largest freezers he'd ever seen. He spread his arms wide. "Food from around the world!"

Some of the other people in the aisle sent him curious looks and hurried away.

Wearing a patient smile, Megan nodded. "It's easy to take so much of this for granted. We can have whatever we want, any time of year."

"Look at this!" He pulled out a cold box from

the freezer and examined the picture on its front. "Macaroni and cheese! Ready in mere minutes."

"I should hope so." She plucked the box from his hands and dropped it into the cart. "I live on this stuff, especially when I'm too tired to cook. But let's get you stocked up, since you'll have a kitchenette and it's a week until payday."

Charles lost his breath when he and Megan turned down another aisle and were presented with open bins full of produce.

"This is a cornucopia!" He gripped a head of lettuce. "How is it possible to have such things in the dead of winter?"

"The wonders of modern technology. Wait until I tell you about the internet."

"The interwhat?"

She shook her head. "We'd better slow this down. Just grab a few things you like to cook."

"I...uh..." He cleared his throat, feeling suddenly abashed. "I don't know how to cook." He felt obliged to explain, "In my youth, before I could afford a household staff, I lived in boarding houses where the food was provided, albeit sparingly. When I earned my fortune, I hired a cook. Most respectable bachelors had them."

"Nice life." She chuckled. "But not too many of us bachelors and spinsters have cooks now." She spun the cart around. "Maybe we should reconsider the frozen food aisle. I can show you how to use a microwave later. And no, I don't know how microwaves work, I just know they heat up my mac and cheese."

"Very good."

After filling the cart with many of the boxes from the aisle with the enormous freezers—including cylindrical items Megan called *burritos*—and various objects for personal hygiene, they approached the cashier.

The entire process fascinated Charles. Megan set items on a small conveyor belt, and the cashier picked each one up and pulled it across a glass panel. As each item moved over the panel, a beep sounded, and a screen similar to the mobile telephone displayed the item and its price. He still could not acclimate himself to the cost of goods in this era, though, and had to remind himself that naturally, there would be inflation. And naturally, he would reimburse Megan for everything.

"How does this work?" he asked Megan.

She held up one of the burritos and pointed to a small series of lines printed on its wrapper. "This is a barcode. The scanner reads the barcode and the information is sent to the cash register."

"But—"

A woman standing behind them in line coughed and sent them both a pointed look, gesturing to the other side of the register where the cashier waited to accept payment. She did not appear happy that Charles wanted to learn about the supermarket's astonishing technology rather than finishing his purchase and moving the line forward.

Charles heaved a sigh. "I'm sorry. I know I'm being tedious."

"It's okay." Megan sent the customer an apologetic look. "He's from a very isolated, rural place. This is all new to him."

The woman nodded, but she did not seem particularly pleased that Charles was preventing her from buying a flat box that read PIZZA.

Megan used a small card made of some variety of celluloid to pay—again, with him insisting that he'd compensate her. It was much less complicated to pay his own way than rely on anyone.

He pointed to the card. "Is that currency?"

"Of a sort. Looks like someone behind us in line has ice cream, and we don't want it to melt while I explain how debit and credit cards work. But I will explain."

Once they'd paid for the food, Megan said to the cashier and the customer, "Merry Christmas! Thanks for your patience."

"Thank *you* for being so patient with me," Charles said as they walked to her automobile. He paused beside her vehicle. "I'm not used to relying on others. It doesn't come easily to me."

"Everyone has times when they need others," she said. The light that illuminated the area where the automobiles were parked shined down on her, making her appear almost angelic.

"I have tried to keep those times to a minimum."

"It's okay to make an exception now and then. I don't think people were meant to be entirely alone." A shadow crossed her face, but she shook her head and the shadow disappeared.

"Perhaps so. You've been extremely helpful, and I'd be in a world of trouble without you."

"I'm happy to help," she said softly. "You've traveled over a hundred years into the future. That's not an easy thing to deal with. And besides," she added as she opened the back of her vehicle and deposited the paper bags inside it, "it's Christmas. Everyone gets an extra helping of kindness at Christmas."

CHAPTER SIX

Megan and Charles carried his groceries down the hallway of the mansion. Everyone had gone home long ago, but the lights were still on, and the tinsel and glass holiday ornaments twinkled cheerfully.

Normally, Megan avoided being alone at the mansion. When it was empty, the huge expanse of house all around her was slightly unnerving. Tonight, however, she was with Charles, and the massive home was softened by all the Christmas cheer surrounding them.

"Is all this really necessary?" Charles grumbled, glancing at a wreath on a door.

"Don't you like it?"

He'd made similar comments in the car, complaining about the amount of Christmas décor in town. As if he resented anything that had to do with the holiday.

"It's rather…excessive."

They moved into the modern section of the house,

and walked into the kitchenette. The wing of the house that had been most personal to Charles had been preserved after his disappearance as per his will, allowing it to be perfectly preserved as a museum—but the rest of the building had become a family home for many years. The family had renovated that portion of the house over the decades, but as of ten years ago, they'd moved out. Now they split their time between Manhattan and Saratoga Springs, though every now and again a member of the family would stop by the mansion just to check in and say hello.

Charles helped unpack the grocery bags while Megan put everything away. Interesting how easily they had fallen into a rhythm. Despite the incredible fact that she'd been born a hundred years after him, they got along so well. She and Brandon had never reached a point in their relationship where they could run errands and just comfortably *be* together without any friction or conflict.

But in the few hours she'd spent with Charles, Megan felt relaxed and contented, like she'd known him all her life.

Get a grip. You're probably still crushing on the Charles from the photograph, not the real *Charles.*

"Seems a little weird that you're grumpy about the decorations," she said, setting a carton of orange juice in the fridge. "Especially considering that every year, you threw a huge Christmas party for your employees at the Belham Hotel."

"Yes, but I never actually attended."

That was news to her. None of the papers or letters she'd read had ever said anything about his non-attendance.

"Why not?"

He paused in the middle of putting a loaf of sliced bread in the cupboard. "Holiday gatherings make me…uncomfortable."

"I'm sorry." She faced him. "Is there something about Christmas that makes you feel that way?"

"Ever since I lost my parents, I stopped caring about the holiday." His expression grew distant. "I remember my first Christmas without them. I was living at a boarding house and the woman who ran it tried to make the place festive with a few bows and garlands. She planned a meal for the boarders with a roast goose and chestnut stuffing. The thought of sitting at that table with strangers, pretending that we meant something to each other…it was too painful. So when my supervisor at the mill said there was work available on Christmas, I jumped at the chance rather than face that boarding house dinner."

Her chest ached at the melancholy image of young Charles, working away at a mill to keep himself from feeling hurt.

"Oh, Charles," she murmured.

"After that, I made a point of working every Christmas. It kept those emotions at bay."

"But it didn't get rid of those feelings. It just set them aside."

His mouth turned downward, and his gaze stayed

on the floor. Then he visibly shook off the emotion, the way someone threw off a heavy and smothering coat.

"Besides," he said with a shrug, "there's always so much to do. So much to plan."

"Yet things must have been different when Eliza came into the picture," Megan felt obligated to point out. "She became your family. I'm sure you celebrated with her, right?"

"Actually…" He fiddled with an apple. "Just before I traveled in time, she wanted me to spend Christmas with her and her family."

"Right!"

"I declined."

Her heart sank.

"I'd read Eliza's letter," she said. "Because history records that you disappeared just after you received it, no one knew that you weren't going to visit her for the holiday."

Megan leaned against the counter and studied him. Sadness settled over her at Charles's confession.

"It's such a wonderful time of year. I'm sorry you denied yourself."

His brow furrowed in thought, and he was silent for a moment.

"I've been thinking about Eliza, actually," he said. "I left her behind in 1902, but I wish I knew what happened to her. I hope she had a happy life."

Uh-oh. Megan bit her lip. How was she supposed to break the news to him about Eliza's marriage to his rival? It wasn't going to be pretty when she finally did. The question was, when should she tell him about Eliza's life after his disappearance?

"I should get going," she said instead. "Tomorrow's a work day. Do you think you'll be okay tonight?"

"Thanks to you, I have everything I need." He smiled and her belly fluttered in response.

"Call me if you need anything at all."

"I will."

They stood awkwardly in the kitchenette, and she wasn't sure if she should hug him or shake his hand, or even do anything at all. She and Charles didn't know each other that well, and manners were different back in his era. Finally, she settled on a friendly wave.

"Have a good night," she said.

"You, as well."

She hurried out of the kitchenette and down the hall, with the emptiness of the house all around her. Quickly, she went outside to her car. As she pulled out her keys, she gave a long exhale, her breath misting in the chill winter air and her heart pounding.

She already liked Charles too much and savored the way he seemed to enjoy her company, but what would he think of her when he realized that she'd withheld some facts from him? When the time came for him to discover that truth, she hoped he'd find a way to forgive not just Eliza, but Megan, too.

Megan sat in her bed, propped against a pile of pillows,

with her historical romance. All the lights were out except her bedside lamp. Reading before going to sleep always relaxed her and let her unwind from a full day.

Tonight, it didn't seem to be working. After fifteen minutes without turning a page, she set the book aside. Engrossing as it was, she couldn't quite focus on reading.

How could she? *Charles Whitley himself* was within a ten-minute drive, and it was all she could do not to pester him with questions about life at the turn of the century. About what it actually felt like to be alive back then, from the smallest detail like taking a bath to the biggest concepts, like watching the world shift from horse-drawn vehicles to automobiles powered by internal combustion engines.

Having him in her time was a historian's dream come true.

But she had to remember that he wasn't a walking, talking history textbook. He was a person. He had the same needs, wants, fears, and joys as anybody else. She'd seen the desolation on his face when he'd realized how alone he was in this era, and also his sadness when talking about spending Christmas without any family.

While he was here, he needed someone to help him find his way in the twenty-first century. He needed an ally.

She would be that for him.

Her phone rang, and she jumped. Immediately, her thoughts went to disasters. Who would call at this late hour without bearing bad news?

Picking up her phone, she breathed in relief when she saw that it wasn't her parents or brother. But her calm didn't last when the screen read *Charles W.*

"Is everything all right, Charles?" she asked when she answered.

"How did you know it was me?"

"I've got you entered into my phone, just like I'm in yours. When the phone rang, the screen displayed your name."

"Ah, yes." His voice grew a little distant as it sounded as though he was holding it away from his face. "I see that now."

"Is everything okay?" she repeated.

"Yes!" he said quickly. "I apologize for the lateness of the hour. Did I wake you?"

"No, it's fine."

"I hope I didn't disturb you in the middle of anything."

Megan glanced down at herself. She wore an oversized T-shirt from the university and baggy pajama pants. Half of a sandwich cookie lay on a napkin atop her nightstand.

Yep, she sure had an exciting life.

"You didn't. Are you sure nothing is wrong?"

"Nothing's *wrong*, precisely."

She heard the uncertainty in his voice. "But…?"

"I'm too excited to sleep," he said with the enthusiasm of a boy. "Here I am, *in the twenty-first century.* I used to dream about what life would be like over a hundred years in the future. It's marvelous, honestly marvelous."

What a unique opportunity for both of them, to learn about the past and, in his case, the future.

It didn't hurt that she genuinely liked Charles. Spending time talking with him wasn't a hardship—it was the opposite of a hardship, in fact.

"Does it meet your expectations?" she asked.

"Yes, and no. In some ways, it doesn't matter whether we can fly using mechanical wings or if we can communicate with each other at any hour, in any place, using miniscule devices. People remain people, no matter what era they live in."

"That's funny—I was just thinking the same thing."

He chuckled softly and it felt like wrapping herself in a snuggly blanket.

"Though I said it before," he murmured, "I just want to thank you again for your kindness. I'm certain I can be tedious with my questions, and my rather…peevish feelings about Christmas, but you've never expressed any impatience, and I'm grateful for everything you have done for me."

"Truly, it's no trouble, Charles." She meant what she said. It cost her nothing to be patient and caring. "I bet if our situations were reversed, you'd be just as compassionate."

"I'm not so certain," he said ruefully. "I wasn't exactly the most easy-tempered man."

"I wouldn't have guessed. Don't forget, I've read

your journals and letters. It's true that you had been very driven," she said, "but you weren't unkind or self-serving like a lot of people in similar situations. Heck, Jay Gould disrupted the entire country's economy just to make himself richer."

"I should hope that I'm not lumped in the same category as the Mephistopheles of Wall Street!"

"You aren't," she quickly assured him.

"The past doesn't really matter in this moment, though." His voice had turned slightly melancholy. "I'm here. Now. And I'm so very indebted to you for all that you've done. Before you can tell me what you're doing is nothing special," he said ahead of her, "not everyone would do the same. So, please accept my gratitude."

"You're very welcome."

There was a long silence, and she pictured him on the other end of the line, a man out of his own time, knowing hardly anyone, separated from everything he used to identify himself. Her heart throbbed with the loss he surely felt.

"I won't disturb your rest any longer," he said, breaking the quiet. "Will I see you tomorrow?"

"Count on it."

"Wonderful. Good night, Megan."

"Good night, Charles. Don't forget to charge your phone."

"Thank you for the reminder. It's just another thing I'll have to grow accustomed to."

Then, like two teenagers, they both stayed on

the line for a long moment, listening to each other breathe, before she finally hung up. She plugged her phone in to charge, and then turned out the light and snuggled down in bed. But she knew it would be hours before she could fall asleep.

Though Megan didn't need to be at the mansion for a while, she showed up hours before she had to lead the first tour.

Dressed in her modern clothes but carrying her "Rosie" costume in a garment bag, she entered the staff room, intending to make herself a cup of tea. To her surprise, Charles was already there, examining the electric kettle. He looked slightly rumpled, and she realized they were going to have to find him more clothes.

"Everywhere I look," he said as she came in, "I find new marvels."

"I'm so used to having modern conveniences, I take them for granted." She plucked a box of her favorite tea down from the cabinet. "Christmas Spice tea?"

He raised an eyebrow. "Even the tea is Christmas?"

"Just try it." She took down two mugs and put the tea bags in them, then filled the kettle before turning it on. "How was your first night's sleep in the twenty-first century?"

"Actually, I didn't sleep at all." He waved away her sound of concern. "I spent most of the night watching television and learning about this new world. Did you know," he said, folding his arms across his chest and leaning against the nearby counter, "that people are using money that doesn't exist? Something called 'Bitecoin?'"

"Bitcoin," she said and smiled. "The gold standard was abandoned in 1933, and the link between the dollar and gold was severed in 1971."

He put a hand to his forehead. "Now money isn't even money. How does one navigate such a world?"

"Don't worry." She put a hand on his arm. "I promise you'll get used to it."

They both noticed her touching him, and she pulled away, fighting to keep from blushing. Fortunately, the kettle worked quickly, and she was able to busy herself pouring hot water over the tea bags. Fragrant spices wafted up, warming her.

She held one mug out to him. He eyed it warily.

Finally, he took the mug from her and sipped. His expression shifted from cautious to pleasantly surprised.

"This is quite good," he said.

"Maybe we can get you on the Christmas train, after all."

"Let's not get ahead of ourselves. Just because I enjoy Christmas Spice tea doesn't mean I intend to play the role of Santa Claus in the town pageant."

"Oh, I don't know." She smiled over the rim of her mug. "You'd look cute in a red velvet hat."

He scowled, but spoiled the look by grinning a moment later.

"Hey, Megan," Amber said as she strode into the break room. She looked at Charles with curiosity. "So you're our new Charles Whitley. Phillip texted me about you. I didn't catch your name."

"Charles," he said, extending his hand.

Amber shook it. "Funny coincidence, playing a man with your name."

"Yes, it is a funny coincidence," he replied.

"Sorry I didn't get a chance to meet you last night. I had to run to the theater as soon as the last tour here was done to make my curtain call. Oh, hey," Amber said to Megan, "if you want, you can let me know if you're planning to see the show, and what night you plan on going. I'll have the house manager save you a seat. Or," she added, glancing at Charles, "two seats."

"That would be great," Megan said. "Thanks."

Amber checked her watch. As she did, the bag she carried shifted and something fell out of it, but she didn't notice. "Oh, shoot. I'm supposed to make a phone call in a minute. Gotta go!"

Before Megan could point out that Amber had dropped something, she spun on her heel and hurried out of the room.

Megan bent down and grabbed the fallen item—which turned out to be a paperback book. *100 Knock-'Em-Dead Audition Monologues* was emblazoned on the cover, and written beneath that in ballpoint pen was a circle surrounding the numbers *12/23!!!*

"That's strange," Megan murmured. "She hasn't

said anything about an audition, especially not in the middle of a show's run."

"Is she usually private about her acting endeavors?" Charles asked. "Perhaps she's shamefaced about pursuing such a disreputable profession."

"We don't have the same feelings about actors that you did back in 1902." She chuckled. "Some of the most revered people in the world are actors."

"Truly?"

"We pay them a lot of money and give them awards."

Charles shook his head. "In my time, some people considered them barely more respectable than hooligans. What a topsy-turvy world this is."

"Good morning, Megan!" Dan came into the break room, carrying his butler costume. Sophia trotted beside him. His gaze frosted when he saw Charles. "Mr. Whitley," he said, his words verging on sarcastic.

"Hi, Dan," Megan said. "Heya, Sophia."

The little girl waved her hello.

"Sir," Charles replied coolly.

"Hi, Mr. Whitley," Sophia said.

Charles's smile for the girl was genuine. "Good morning, Sophia."

Sophia went to the small fridge and pulled out a cup of yogurt. As she did so, Dan eyed Charles.

"You know, of course," Dan said, "that the real Charles Whitley would never wear wrinkled clothing. He was a self-made man, and took great pride in his appearance."

95

"I did, and I do," Charles said, drawing himself up. "Unfortunately, my valet probably passed away seventy years ago."

Dan rolled his eyes. "Maybe it's time to dial back the method acting."

"Okay, okay." Megan held up her hands, urging calm. "It's early in the morning, and Christmas is in five days, so maybe we ought to just take a breath and try to be kind to each other."

How was she supposed to explain to Dan that Charles was *actually* Charles? Even an astrophysicist would struggle with that task.

At that moment, Phillip strolled in, looking very festive in a seasonal sweater.

"Morning, everyone!" Phillip said. "Is everyone prepared for our big Whitley-Moran Mansion Christmas party?"

Frowning, Charles set his mug down.

"Why," he said in a low voice, "are you referring to my house as the Whitley-Moran Mansion? Harold Moran was my *rival*. What does he have to do with my home?"

Charles looked at Megan.

She swallowed hard. There would be no hiding the truth from Charles. She just hoped he wouldn't hold it against her.

CHAPTER SEVEN

The stricken look on Megan's face made Charles's stomach knot in apprehension. She had such an open, sincere air and was usually quick to smile. That made her clear discomfort and…guilt?…seem all the more alarming.

The room had also gone quite silent.

"Well," she said, then cleared her throat, "after your disappearance, Eliza took possession of the house."

"Naturally," he said. "My solicitor's instructions were quite clear on that point. It was always meant for her, so long as she respected my desire to have some rooms open to the public."

"She preserved the wing where you lived and worked, just as you'd wanted. But, um…" Megan looked away. "About eight months after you disappeared, she married."

"I see." It wasn't pleasant to hear, but it wasn't entirely surprising. Eliza was a lovely girl from an esteemed family. It stood to reason that she would eventually find someone else to marry. "Who was her husband?"

Megan grimaced. "Harold Moran."

The floor fell away from beneath Charles's feet. "…What?"

"He courted her pretty intensely," Megan said, "and it worked. After they married, they moved into the mansion together. They had four children, and about ten years ago, their descendants left the house to the town of Cutter Springs to take over running the museum."

"I…"

Charles had, back in his time, visited a pugilism academy several times a week to keep his body as sharp as his mind. Occasionally, his instructor had managed to punch him right in the chest.

He felt like that now: as though he'd collided with a massive fist and couldn't get enough air. He pressed his hand to the counter, trying to steady himself, seeking solidity in the feel of the laminated wood against his palm.

How? How was this possible?

"Do you mean to tell me," he said, barely able to speak, "that scalawag Harold Moran had the life I was meant to have?"

"Charles—"

His head whipped up as he stared at Megan. "You knew. All this time, you knew, and you didn't tell me."

"I'm sorry."

But he couldn't hear her right now. He needed to move, to think.

Charles stalked from the break room, dodging around Amber as she came back into the chamber. Behind him, he heard Sophia say, "Daddy, there's something I have to tell you."

Moving through his house with its festive décor only struck Charles all the harder. This had been his private sanctuary, a place he'd designed to start a life with Eliza, but all his plans had been cruelly turned upside down. Again and again through his life, he faced loss, beginning with the loss of his parents when he was little more than a child.

Now he'd lost the life he had intended.

He stormed into his study and braced his hands on the bookshelves.

"Charles," Megan said behind him.

"I don't think it's possible for me to communicate to you how much I loathed Moran," he said, feeling his words choke in his throat. "At every turn in my life, he plagued me, mocking me because I wasn't born into wealth and privilege. And now I learn that not only did he take over my home, he married my fiancée."

"I'm so sorry for not telling you earlier. I was afraid of this very reaction." Her voice was full of genuine contrition.

"You should have said something sooner."

"You're right. I should have."

It wasn't fair to be angry with Megan. She'd only been protecting him from a truth she knew would devastate him. The brunt of his fury was for Moran, not her.

"I'm mostly upset that Moran got everything that was supposed to be mine. He took the future I wanted." Charles turned around to face her. "That's the most difficult part."

"I understand."

Suddenly, he knew precisely what needed to happen.

Everything fell into place, and he felt the way he did when solving a particularly thorny engineering problem.

"There's only one thing to do," he said.

"What's that?"

"Now it's imperative that I find a way back to my time."

Megan stared at him, her eyes wide. After a moment, she said, "But how?"

Before he could answer her question, Phillip, Dan, Sophia, and Amber came into the room, all wearing expressions of concern.

"Is everything okay?" Phillip asked.

Charles immediately knelt on the floor and moved the panel in the floorboards. He exhaled in relief when he found his journal still there. The pages had gone yellow and brittle with time, but no insects had eaten them.

"Oh, my goodness," Phillip said in a whisper.

Amber looked at Sophia. "You were telling the truth. He really *is* Charles Whitley."

The little girl looked vindicated. "I know."

"*That's* why you disappeared," Amber breathed. "Because you traveled to *now*."

"Heck," Dan said, his face chalky. "I…criticized you. For not being good at being yourself."

Seeing the mortification on Dan's face made any of Charles's lingering resentment flee.

"No harm," Charles said. "I understand what it means to have pride in your work. Hopefully, we can be friends." He crouched down to put himself at Sophia's eye level. "You're a very clever girl."

"That's true," Sophia said with a nod.

"Can you help me figure out how I wound up here in your time? Maybe if we can discover the means by which I traveled here in the first place, we can recreate it, and I can go home."

"You want me to help?" Her eyes went round.

"I think you're the perfect person for the job." He handed her the journal. "This belonged to me. There might be clues in here that I can't recall."

Sophia wrapped her arms around it as though it was the most precious thing in the world.

"Thank you, Mr. Whitley. I'll get to work right away. Let's go back to the break room, Daddy." She walked out quickly, with Dan, Phillip, and Amber following.

Charles straightened, and when he looked at Megan, her eyes were sad.

"Sounds like you're pretty determined to get back to 1902," she said, her smile slightly melancholy.

"What about all the modern technology you find so exciting?"

"Beating Moran at his own game takes priority over mobile telephones and burritos."

Urgency and the need to best his rival burned at him. Harold Moran had always struck him as too superior, too convinced of his own opinion. Moran always had a group of flunkies around him, laughing too loudly at his jokes and sneering at people Moran disliked.

Moran had never made a secret of his scorn for Charles's humble background, either. In the press, he'd called Charles, *That mill worker*, rather than refer to Charles by name. There had also been that time when Charles had dined with business associates at Delmonico's, and when he'd been shown to a table that was right next to Moran's, the insufferable man had gotten up and demanded to be moved.

"Someplace where I can't smell the stink of iron ore," Moran had declared loudly.

And for Moran to live in Charles's *house*, to marry Charles's *fiancée*?

Intolerable.

"It might take a little while to figure out how to get you home," Megan said.

"It might. But when I set my mind to something, I labor very hard to make it happen."

"Maybe," she said slowly, "while you're working on that, you can enjoy the Christmas season, too."

Her words struck him hard, and he ducked his head.

"In truth, I'm not very good at what you'd call 'enjoying the moment.' Even on my trips abroad, I filled my journals with ideas about business, not impressions of where I went."

"I know," she said gently. "I've read them. They're part of the house's collection."

He walked to the fireplace and looked down into it. Someone had lit the fire—presumably Phillip—and it crackled cheerfully in counterpart to his low mood.

"I've been to London, Paris, Berlin," he said. "But I barely remember anything about those places."

His heart felt heavy as he tried to recall what he'd eaten for breakfast when he'd stayed in a luxury hotel near the Place Vendôme, and remembered…nothing. He didn't remember the view out his window, and he had no impressions of the trees or the river or anything at all. It was as though he'd been drifting through life, stuck in his head.

"I've got an idea," Megan said, breaking through his thoughts. "It's my job to tell people how Christmas was celebrated in the past. Maybe…I can continue to be your tour guide, and show you how we celebrate Christmas now."

Her smile was unsure, but her eyes were bright.

His first impulse was to politely decline. He'd simply be too busy researching how to return to 1902 to waste time with frivolous things like evergreen wreaths and whatever else people did to observe the holiday.

But time travel was not precisely his area of expertise. Perhaps, while he attempted to sift through this complex and murky subject, he could do as Megan suggested. There was a world of experiences and knowledge that he didn't possess. As long as he was here in the future, he could explore what it meant to stop and look around. Perhaps this sojourn in this era could help him in that goal.

And…he enjoyed spending time with Megan.

"I like your notion," he said, and her smile became fuller. "A Christmas adventure."

They grinned at each other, until Phillip poked his head into the study.

"Hey, guys, our first tour starts in thirty minutes, and I'm going to need everyone in costume and at their places. Folks yesterday really liked it when you pretended to be shocked by them being in your house, so maybe more of that. I think we'll keep you in the study instead of the ballroom, too, so we get more of that back-and-forth with Megan. Speaking of which," Phillip added, "Megan, give him a copy of the script so he knows what info he needs to tell our visitors."

"Sure—there's one in the break room." She glanced at Charles. "Can you memorize it in thirty minutes?"

"I believe so," he answered, hoping that his voice conveyed more certainty than he felt.

"Thanks! Oh, and for now, we'll pay you under

the table. Since it might be a little difficult to explain to the government how we're paying a time traveler." Phillip waved before disappearing.

"Are you up for this?" Megan asked with concern.

He drew a breath. "I think I am. It will be quite novel to play myself. What do you think if I say something like, 'If you rapscallions do not vacate my premises immediately, I shall summon the police! See if I don't!'"

Megan laughed. "I like it. It's just snooty enough."

"Miss Turner," he said as arrogantly as possible, "I am not 'snooty,' I'm 'confident.'"

They both laughed.

"Let me get the script." She hurried out, but returned a moment later with a thin sheaf of paper. "This is it. You can improvise, but these are the basic facts we want our visitors to know."

He snorted softly as he thumbed through the pages. Here it was, the sum of his life's story, right here in his hands. It felt as though he looked at himself in a mirror in another room.

"Should we rehearse a little of what we're going to say?" Megan asked.

"I think that would be best."

For the next few minutes, they went back and forth with lines that they each suggested, until they were satisfied with the results. Charles felt slightly awkward at first, but Megan was so calm, so comfortable and ready with her smile, that soon he lost his self-consciousness.

At last, it was time to let visitors in.

"Have fun today," Megan said, walking to the door of his study.

"I will." And for the first time, he truly believed it.

CHAPTER EIGHT

Wearing her Rosie costume, Megan escorted visitors into Charles's study. She smoothed her hands down her apron, trying to calm her nerves. This was Charles's first official appearance as "Charles Whitley." Would he be successful at it when he had to perform it as a role, or would he crumple? Not everyone was cut out to be a reenactor, which she'd seen before with other staff members who quickly flamed out.

After Megan had rehearsed with Charles, it was finally time to put him to the test.

"Right this way, everyone," she said. "I'm sure Mr. Whitley won't mind if we have a look in his study."

"I should say I do mind," Charles exclaimed from behind his desk.

"Oh, Mr. Whitley," Megan said, feigning surprise. "I didn't realize you were in here."

He stood. "What do you mean by bringing all

these peculiarly dressed strangers into my private study, Rosie?"

"They're only here to admire your lovely home. Isn't that right, friends?" She turned to the guests, who were smiling broadly and filming the interaction on their phones.

Some people nodded at her prompting look.

"If you rapscallions do not vacate my premises immediately," Charles said hotly, "I shall summon the police! See if I don't!"

"It's Christmas, Mr. Whitley," Megan beseeched. "No one wants to be taken in by the police so close to the holiday."

"Very well," he grumbled. "You may look about, but keep it brief." He walked around his desk and leaned against it, his arms folded across his chest.

Megan pointed out the noteworthy aspects of the study, as she had before, but soon she turned to Charles.

"Might I impose upon you to answer a few of our guests' questions?"

"Very well," he said in a reluctant voice.

For a moment, the visitors were silent, likely a bit intimidated by the commanding presence of Mr. Whitley. Finally, one girl wearing glasses nervously raised her hand.

"Yes, miss?" Charles asked, his voice much more friendly.

"Where do you get your ideas from?" she asked.

Charles rubbed a hand along his jaw. "A very good

question. I wish I could say I have a reliable source of inspiration, but it's nearly impossible for me to predict what will make my mind start turning. Sometimes, it's the way the light hits a piece of metal. Other times, I'll see someone struggling to complete a task, and will think about how I could make their work easier or faster. It's quite variable."

Girl in glasses nodded. "Thanks."

"Of course," he answered, his tone sincere and kind.

Megan warmed to see how he treated the girl, putting her at ease and speaking to her with respect. His answer had been detailed and thoughtful, too, and not a bit dismissive.

A man with a cane raised his hand.

"Yes, sir?" Charles asked.

"How long does it take you to create a new invention?"

"Another excellent question." Charles's forehead wrinkled in thought. "It can take anywhere from a week to a year, depending on the length of time I need to formulate the concept, create prototypes, test the prototypes, and then apply for a patent. At any given time, I'm working on several concepts at once, all of them at different stages of development, so it's a challenge to keep everything straight."

"That's where I come in," Megan said. "I keep the house running, and ensure that Mr. Whitley is organized. Without me reminding him, he wouldn't eat and would skip sleep entirely."

"Yes, Rosie, you are indispensable," Charles said grudgingly after rolling his eyes. "How would I ever remember which shoe goes on which foot?"

"You wouldn't, if I didn't write *left* and *right* on them."

The guests chuckled, and a little firework display of happiness popped and fizzed in Megan's chest. Most of this back-and-forth with Charles was pure improvisation, and it felt so good to have someone with whom she could be so in tune. She and Charles played naturally off of each other.

She caught herself looking at Charles a bit too long, and reminded herself that he was only here for a short while. He was determined to return to 1902, and Eliza.

But he's here now, so let's make it good for him.

A tall man in a sweatshirt with a football team's logo on it spoke. "Aren't you less significant than Henry Ford?"

Megan frowned at the man's rude question.

"Had I not disappeared," Charles said in an even and measured tone, "I surely would have invented the moving assembly line long before Ford did."

"But you were only doing your thing for a decade," the man pressed. "Ford was around for half a century."

"Precisely," Charles said. "I did much more in a short amount of time than Ford accomplished in fifty years. Besides, it's the quality of how one spends one's time, rather than the length of time you're given."

"I think we've imposed on Mr. Whitley long

enough," Megan said, eager to keep the interactions pleasant. "We'll continue our tour."

When the last visitor left the study, Megan smiled and gave him a thumbs-up. He returned the gesture, his own smile wide and genuine.

The same pattern repeated for the second tour, with Charles acting grumpy upon their entrance, but then being very patient and kind with the visitors when they asked questions. He was especially gentle with the children. Again, Megan and Charles bantered, to the delight of the guests—and Megan herself. It felt right and natural to be with him like this, and she could hardly believe that she and Charles hadn't been doing this together forever.

When the final guests left the mansion at five o'clock, Megan went into the break room and found Charles poring over a newspaper. He looked up as she entered and gave her a wave.

"How did your first day playing 'Charles Whitley' go?" she asked.

"Marvelously well, I think," he answered. "The visitors certainly kept me on my toes."

"But you were very good with them."

"Curiosity should always be encouraged."

Megan nodded. "No doubt."

Amber strolled into the break room, still wearing her costume. She walked to the cabinet to grab a mug.

"The guests kept telling me how great 'Mr. Whitley' was," she said with a wink. "They were getting angry with me for marrying Moran."

Charles grumbled under his breath.

"I think you're a hit," Amber said quickly in a clear effort to change the topic from Harold Moran.

"That's very kind," Charles said.

Megan pulled the book of audition monologues from her cubby and brought it to Amber.

"I think you dropped this earlier."

A blush spread across Amber's cheeks as she quickly took the book. "Thanks." Setting down the mug, she hurried to her own cubby and stuffed the book into her bag.

"Are you planning on auditioning for anything?" Megan asked.

"Um, well…" Amber fidgeted with the lace on her cuff. "There's an original play going up on Broadway this season. The playwright won a Tony a couple of years ago. Everyone in the New York acting scene wants a part. People are supposed to send in their audition videos by December twenty-third."

"How exciting!" Charles said. "Are you going to do it?"

Amber's eyes flicked downward. "Not sure."

"Why not?" Megan wondered.

"It's just…" Amber shrugged. "It's a really big deal, and maybe I'm not good enough. I just do regional theater, not big Broadway productions. The best of the best are trying out for roles."

"Amber," Megan said, setting her hand on her friend's arm, "I've seen you act, ever since we were in the middle school production of *Alice in Wonderland*.

You stole the show as the Queen of Hearts. You should go for it."

"Maybe. I don't know." Amber glanced away again. "I have to go. The show starts in a little bit, and I need to grab a quick dinner before my call time."

Before Megan could press the issue any further, Amber took her bag and walked quickly from the room.

Megan exhaled. "I really want this for Amber, but it's tough to get her to see how much she deserves it."

"If she's ambitious," Charles said, "then she needs to take the risk."

A wave of nervousness came over Megan. He'd come from humble origins, and he'd toiled hard to elevate himself. But how would he feel about the bag of secondhand clothes she'd gotten for him? He kept insisting on paying her back for his groceries and phone, but maybe borrowed clothing would be too much for him to accept. Charles definitely had pride, and wasn't the sort of person who easily accepted a handout.

"I, um, have something for you."

"Oh?"

She went to the cubby that served as her locker and retrieved a large shopping bag, then walked the bag over to him.

"Payday's not for a week," she said, "and I thought you might need some other clothing, and a warm coat."

He peered inside and pulled out a pair of jeans. "Denim trousers—we wore these in the steel mill."

"Everybody wears them now, and they last a long time."

He pulled out a few sweaters, shirts, and a coat, which he arranged on the dining table. They were in an array of handsome, deep colors that would suit Charles perfectly.

"I called my mom and she brought by some of my brother's stuff," Megan said. "You're around the same size as Nate."

"Won't he miss all this?"

"Nathan? He's a clotheshorse and every time he comes for a visit, he leaves stuff behind, so I thought…" She shrugged and looked at him uncertainly. "I hope you don't mind."

Charles made a small, thoughtful sound. "When I made my first thousand dollars, I commissioned a wardrobe from Manhattan's finest tailors and haberdashers. I never thought I'd be in a place in my life where I'd rely on castoff garments again."

"It's just a loan," she said. "Except for the, uh, socks and underwear. That's all new. You'll give the rest back when you have enough to buy your own clothes."

"Of course I will," he said at once. He held up a navy sweater to his shoulders. "This should suit me well enough. Thank you."

"Sure. And maybe you could wear your warmest stuff for our outing tonight."

"What is tonight?"

"The town tree-lighting ceremony. Before you say no," she said hastily, seeing he was about to do just that, "remember what we talked about earlier? How you might be able to use this time to experience life more? Well, now's your chance."

He still looked doubtful. "I don't know…"

"Come on." She playfully tugged on his sleeve. "It's just a few minutes, and if you hate it, I'll take you right back home again. Don't forget—I'm your Christmas guide. I *promise* you'll have fun."

She wasn't certain why it was so important to her that Charles finally experience the magic of the season, but the thought of him returning to 1902 without seeing how wonderful Christmas could be made her heart heavy. His life had been one of work and ambition but hardly any feeling. She wanted to give him a bit of Christmas cheer.

"All right," he said after a moment. "But before we go, I need to spend some time researching my disappearance. I feel certain that there must be a clue in there as to what caused me to travel through time. If I know that, then perhaps I'll be able to reproduce the conditions and return home." He scowled. "The very idea that Moran took over my life makes my blood boil. I *must* prevent his appropriation of my home and my fiancée from happening."

"Right. Of course." Disappointment flattened her eagerness, but naturally Charles would want to go back to his own time, and back to Eliza. "Maybe I could help."

"Are you certain? It might be rather dull work."

115

She laughed. "I'm an academic, remember? Dull work is exciting to me!"

A corner of his mouth turned up. "Excellent. Shall we reconnoiter in my study in thirty minutes?"

"Sounds good. That'll give us time to change our clothes. And when we're done with our investigation, I'll drive us to Cutter Springs Park for the tree lighting."

"I am looking forward to it—I think."

Back in her daily clothes, Megan strode into the study, then stopped abruptly.

Charles stood by one of the bookcases, a book in his hands. He'd changed into the modern clothing she'd lent him. He wore a dark gray sweater, and slim-cut jeans. With his well-trimmed beard, he looked as though he could have stepped from the pages of an upscale catalogue.

"Uh—wow."

He glanced up from the book, a small line appearing between his eyebrows as he frowned. "Is something wrong?"

"No. Everything's great." She shook her head, trying to clear it. "Where do we start?"

Holding up the book in his hands, he said, "I'm looking into other accounts of time travel. There are several volumes in my library that address the issue. This one has Washington Irving's story, 'Rip Van Winkle.'" He nodded toward his desk, where a small stack of books perched on the edge. "You'll find other texts that address traveling through time."

Megan went to the desk and grabbed the book on top of the stack. She read the spine. "*A Christmas Carol*? Seasonally appropriate. Did you see or talk to any Ghosts of Christmas Future before you jumped forward in time?"

"Not that I'm aware of."

"I think you'd probably notice something like that. Tall guy, black hooded cloak. Doesn't say much." She glanced at him. "We can probably rule that theory out."

Charles nodded, then returned his book to the shelf. "Nor did I fall asleep after meeting mysterious men playing ninepins." He walked to the desk and plucked the next book from the pile. "There are still other avenues to explore. Mark Twain's *A Connecticut Yankee In King Arthur's Court.*"

"Before you time traveled, did you get a blow to the head? That's what happens to Hank Morgan in the book."

"I did not. And in the Yankee's case, he traveled *back* in time."

"So we can probably rule that out."

"There's H.G. Wells's *The Time Machine*, but I didn't invent a massive contraption to speed me to eight hundred thousand years into the future." He made a small grunt of irritation. "Blast. I thought there might be a clue in some of these stories."

She moved to the bookcase and patted a few of the

volumes shelved there. "Much as I love books and a good library, there's a lot more information online."

Another frown pleated his forehead. "*Online*? As in, a telephone line?"

"Sort of." She exhaled. "The internet is basically a telecommunications network that connects people all over the world. Important information is stored there—and a lot of stuff that's a huge waste of time." She thought of the hours she'd spent watching videos of cats playing and recipes for the world's best chocolate chip cookie.

"How do I find it?"

She quickly discarded the idea of using her phone, since it was small and not every website was designed to be seen on mobile devices. "There's a computer in Phillip's office. I don't think he'd mind if we used it. We should find some good info with a few quick searches."

"By all means, let us go." Charles waved her forward, and she saw in the eagerness of his gesture how impatient he was to get answers.

Her heart sank, but she couldn't be saddened that he wanted to go home. At least, she *told* herself not to be sad—but even in the short amount of time she'd been in Charles's company, she'd grown attached.

Megan led him down the hallway, past the rooms open to the public, before heading down a smaller corridor that, in its day, had been used by servants. She opened the door marked *Phillip Tran, Director*, flipped on the light, then went quickly to the desk and turned on the laptop sitting atop it.

"I'm the furthest thing from a computer expert," she explained as Charles stood beside her. "If you want to know how the internet works, you'd be better off going to the university and talking to one of the IT professors."

Charles stared with fascination at the screen before blinking his eyes. "Much as I would love dismantling this device and learning how it functions, I'm more interested right now in what it has to tell us."

"I think Phillip would be a little miffed if you took his computer apart, too." She opened Google and typed *time travel* into the search box. A second later, hundreds of thousands of hits appeared. "Yikes. We've got a ton of stuff to sift through here. Let's try to narrow it down."

"Perhaps other people disappeared the same day I did," Charles suggested. "Perhaps they, too, traveled into the future. We can search for commonalities."

"Fortunately, being an academic has given me a black belt in online research."

Charles glanced at her waist. "What does the color of your belt have to do with conducting research?"

She fought to keep from smiling. "It's a ranking system for people who practice Asian martial arts. I was just being metaphorical." She held up a hand. "Don't worry, Charles. I've got this."

Yet, after a solid hour of research, they were no closer to their goal than they'd been earlier. They had tried examining accounts of disappearances, different geographical locations and their proximity to unexplained events, even folk tales of portals to fairy kingdoms. Nothing yielded results.

As Megan typed, Charles paced back and forth in the small office. The longer they searched, the quicker he moved, until he looked like a pinball ricocheting from one wall to the other.

"We're not getting anywhere," she finally admitted. "I'm sorry."

The look of frustration on his face made her stomach clench. Even so, he said, "We made an attempt. This foray wasn't successful, but I'm not quitting."

"Maybe a tree-lighting ceremony might cheer you up," she said.

His expression shifted to one of doubt. "I'm not certain how."

"Just give it a shot." She stood. "You're a man of science—you know how important it is to conduct experiments. Even those that don't yield the desired result still mean something."

After a moment, he nodded. "All right. Show me this mood-altering tree."

She shut down the computer and turned out the light before they exited the office. A small gleam of happiness shined within her. Much as she wanted to help Charles, it certainly was nice to have him in her time for a little longer.

Bundled into their winter coats, she drove Charles into town, and parked a few blocks away from the center of town.

"Before we go to the tree-lighting ceremony," she said as she locked the car, "there's something I want to show you."

Anticipation nearly made her bounce on her feet like a kid, but she managed to keep it together enough to stay rooted to the ground. She'd also had trouble staying focused after seeing Charles in modern clothing.

"What is it?" he asked.

"A surprise. But one you'll like. I promise." She wasn't actually certain if he'd like what she had in store for them, but she decided to brazen it out. "Come with me."

She mounted the stairs to the library, a two-story structure that boasted neocolonial architecture, complete with columns flanking the entryway.

"We're going to read?" Charles asked.

"You'll see."

They entered the library and were quickly enfolded in the pleasant, cozy hush. Fortunately, the library kept later hours during the holiday season to accommodate kids who were on break from school. A small Christmas tree stood in the entryway, its branches adorned with ornaments that resembled tiny books. Even the angel on top of the tree held a book in her hands.

Megan pointed to the mural that decorated the entryway. In a thick, muscular style, the mural depicted workers operating printing presses and distributing books and newspapers to a grateful populace.

"This is one of the older buildings in town," she said in a quiet voice. "It was completed during the era of the WPA—the Works Progress Administration created by President Roosevelt in the 1930s."

"President Roosevelt was still in office by the '30s?" Charles asked in shock.

"*Franklin* Roosevelt," Megan said. "A distant cousin to Theodore."

"I see." He looked at the mural thoughtfully. "Strange to think that something from the 1930s is considered old. It was decades ahead of me."

"The fact that all this time travel hasn't made you go off your rocker is amazing," Megan said.

A corner of his mouth curved upward. "Outside, I appear calm, but inside, I am a fairground carousel, turning in circles." He looked back at the mural. "Is this what you intended to show me?"

"Nope. Follow me."

They walked past the tall bookshelves that housed Cutter Springs's collection of books. This had been one of Megan's favorite places as a kid. Heck, it still was one of her favorite places. She'd spent many wonderful hours poring through the American History books, learning new details about how people lived in times past. She'd also plowed through the library's romance novels—she never could resist a Happily Ever After.

People worked on computers, and others read at tables or in comfy chairs. A few recognized Megan as she moved past and gave her friendly waves. The children's section had much lower shelves, tables, and chairs, plus play mats spread on the floor so kids could sprawl out as they read. Posters of celebrities encouraging children to read were hung around the kids' section.

Megan and Charles approached the check-out desk, and Mr. Hernandez, the librarian, removed his bifocals and smiled in greeting. On the counter was a tiny evergreen tree, decorated just like its big brother in the entryway.

"Hi, Mr. Hernandez," Megan said in a friendly but quiet voice.

"Hello, Megan."

The librarian glanced at Charles, and Megan quickly made introductions, though she made sure not to give Charles's last name since that might make for a peculiar conversation. The two men shook hands.

"Are you here for the latest releases?" Mr. Hernandez asked. "We just got a new batch of historical romances that I think you'll love."

"Not tonight," she said. "I was wondering if we could go on up?"

Mr. Hernandez gave her a secretive smile. "Going to show your friend the—"

Megan put her finger to her lips. "It's a surprise."

"Of course. Head on upstairs. Here's the key." He plucked a key attached to a book-shaped piece of brass and handed it to Megan. "Have fun."

"Thank you."

"Very nice meeting you," Charles said before he and Megan moved on.

She pushed open the door that led to the staircase. "Ready to climb?"

"Lead on."

At the top of the stairs was the floor of the library that contained the periodicals and media collection. There were fewer people up here, and those that were didn't look up as she and Charles passed. She went toward a door with a ROOF ACCESS sign.

"Almost there," she whispered to Charles as she unlocked the door, revealing a very narrow set of metal stairs.

Their feet clanged on the steps as they went up higher, and at the top, she unlocked another door before pushing it open. It revealed a tar paper-covered expanse, lightly coated with snow, as well as a low railing that ran the perimeter of the roof.

"Here we are." She walked out onto the roof with her arms open.

Charles emerged to stand beside her. They both looked around, taking in the roofline of Cutter Springs and the lights that shined up from the street. The stars appeared a little dimmer in town than back at the mansion, but they still twinkled overhead. Faintly, sounds of traffic below could be heard, and a few voices as pedestrians passed.

"There's the movie theater," Megan said, pointing to the neon marquee. She gestured toward other landmarks. "And the pizza parlor, and the university's office of continuing education."

"A very nice view," Charles said.

"Here's the reason why I brought you up here." She put her hands on his shoulders—ignoring the solid way he felt beneath her gloved hands—and gently turned him. She angled his body in just the right way, until she was satisfied. "Ta-da!"

"What am I looking at?"

"If you look right in this direction," she said, excitement in her voice, "down First Avenue, you can see all the older, historical buildings in Cutter Springs dating from around the turn of the century. It's just like looking back into the past."

The town hall, clock tower, firehouse, and city offices lined the street, their handsome stone facades decorated for the season, like the rest of the town. Had she and Charles been at street level, she could have pointed out the dedication plaques that announced the year the buildings were completed—1903.

"I remember this," he said in a stunned whisper. "I remember all of these structures being built, but construction had stopped for the season."

"Now you get to see what they look like finished."

He walked slowly to the railing and looked out at the scene, an expression of amazement on his face. "This is quite extraordinary. It's almost as if I was back once more."

"If you listen closely," she said, coming to stand

125

beside him, "you can hear the clip-clop of horse hooves and the sputtering of motor cars' engines."

A slow smile spread across his face. "I can almost hear it."

They stood together for several moments, taking in the scene. It was peaceful and restful, and it wasn't difficult to imagine that she and Charles truly had traveled back in time to a simpler era.

"How did you find out about this place?" he asked.

"When I was in high school, Mr. Hernandez noticed me always checking out all the books on late-nineteenth and early-twentieth-century history, so he said I should come up and showed me where to stand in just the right spot." She breathed out into the cool air. "I used to come here a lot, when I was being a moody teen and wanted some space."

With a start, she realized that she'd never brought anyone up here before. She hadn't wanted to share this piece of the past with anyone—not even Brandon. The vantage had been her private getaway. Until now.

It felt right, though, to share it with Charles. He, more than anyone, would understand and appreciate what it meant to see Cutter Springs through the lens of history. He'd recognize the significance of past times, and how everything in the present moment was built upon the past. Only through knowing what had come before could anybody move forward.

"Thank you," he said softly, "for sharing this with me. I'm honored."

His simple, sincere words made heat rush up into her cheeks and her heart beat faster.

"Glad you like it."

"I do. Very much."

She fought the urge to take his hand, although everything in her yelled that she should. Instead, she stuffed her hands into her pockets and stood beside him, feeling comfortable and happy and pleased that he understood what this all meant to her.

Megan said nothing. She just let the moment be.

Though she wanted to linger on the roof with Charles, the tree-lighting ceremony was happening in just a few minutes, and there was no way she wanted him to miss that. They headed back downstairs and gratefully returned the key to Mr. Hernandez before leaving the library.

She and Charles walked to the center of town where many people had gathered. Everyone wore warm coats and hats, their faces glowing in the brisk December air. Megan's pulse skipped to see how festive everything looked—and how nice Charles looked in his modern clothing.

The tree itself stood in a small park in the very middle of town. The Eastern White Pine was almost twenty feet tall. It was in a huge planter, preserving the roots until it would be planted in a nearby forest after the New Year.

"We didn't have this ceremony in my time," Charles

said as he and Megan approached the park. "Has the town always used live trees?"

"Not always. The idea of planting the town's Christmas tree started back in the hippie '60s."

"*Hippie*? Does that involve baby hippopotami?"

She chuckled. "It would be pretty exciting if it did involve huge mammals. I'd love to see elephants and rhinos roaming around Cutter Springs."

"Giraffes acting as traffic signals."

"And if anybody acts up, Police Officer Lion will roar at them!"

They laughed together as they entered the park where the ceremony was set to take place. Though Megan had been to quite a few tree-lighting ceremonies, she never lost her sense of excitement as the magic hour approached. It was even better to share it with Charles.

Much of the town had come out for the event, and a quartet sang carols while some local teens operated a hot cocoa stand, raising funds to upgrade the high school's disability access. Younger children threw snowballs and squealed in shock and delight whenever they got tagged. Their parents and other adults milled around in groups, greeting each other and chattering animatedly in advance of the actual lighting of the tree.

Megan waved at people she knew—from her postal carrier, to the man who bagged her groceries, to friends she'd known since preschool—everyone gathering together to celebrate the season.

Charles took it all in with a curious expression, like someone visiting a strange and distant kingdom.

"The ornaments were all made by local children." She pointed to some of the creations of yarn and construction paper. "There's a contest to see who can design the best tree topper."

"And I won," Sophia said as she skipped up to them. She wore a hat with a large pom-pom, no doubt knitted by her doting grandmother. "But not because my mom is the tree-lighting ceremony director."

"Certainly not," Charles said. He looked up at the pretty star Sophia had constructed of twigs and glittery pipe cleaners. "It's capital!"

The little girl beamed, and her parents approached.

"Nice work today, man," Dan said. He gave Charles's shoulder an amicable punch. "The visitors couldn't stop talking about you."

"It's a group effort," Charles replied with a decisive nod.

"Charles," Dan said, extending a hand. "This is my wife, Lydia."

"Charmed," Charles said with a gentlemanly bow.

Megan fought to keep from sighing. There was something so gallant about Charles's manners that spoke directly to her inner romantic.

"I've heard so much about you," Lydia said. Her lovely dark brown skin was rosy from the cold, and her natural hair puffed out from beneath her hat. She and Megan hugged.

"So this is your doing?" Charles asked as he gazed at the tree.

"I had some help from volunteers," Lydia said, "including a few from my own family." She tapped a finger on a giggling Sophia's nose. "But yes, I'm the madwoman responsible for all this."

Megan tensed. Hopefully, Charles wouldn't say anything too cutting or dismissive about holiday decorations being silly.

"It's truly marvelous," Charles said, his voice sounding sincere.

Megan silently exhaled while Lydia smiled shyly.

"We take our Christmas pretty seriously around here," Dan said, and wrapped an arm around Lydia's shoulders.

Just then, a couple approached and began talking to Lydia and Dan, thanking both of them for their contributions to the town's festivities.

"Mr. Whitley," Sophia said, once her parents were distracted, "I've been looking and looking and can't find anything yet to help you…" She glanced around. "…you know what. But I'll keep searching, I promise."

The little girl's forehead wrinkled. Clearly, she took her assignment seriously.

"You have my gratitude, Miss Sophia," Charles said.

She nodded solemnly before going to her parents and taking their hands.

"Let's take pictures of my star," she said with all the bossiness of a child.

Her parents nodded and ambled off, leaving Megan alone with Charles.

"So…?" she asked. "What do you think?" She spread her arms wide to indicate the townspeople in their coats and scarves, the carolers, the steaming cups of hot cocoa. People posed for photos in front of the tree and playfully kissed beneath a sprig of mistletoe that was tied to a lamppost.

The energy was lively, abundant with Christmas cheer. But maybe Charles thought it all rather silly.

"Those Christmas parties I threw every year for my employees," he said. "I told you how I never went. I knew the holiday mattered to them, but it didn't matter to me. I thought, *I don't like Christmas*, and left it at that."

"That's too bad."

"Yet I wonder if it actually kept me from getting close with anyone," he said softly, as though the idea was only then occurring to him. "It's one thing to interact with people at our places of employment, but socializing outside of the workplace was all but unknown to me. And I put up that same barrier between Eliza and me."

"But she was your fiancée," Megan said, puzzled. "You were close with her, right?"

"Not truly." Sadness weighted his words. "I kept her at a distance—which was entirely my doing."

"I'm so sorry," Megan said, aching for Charles and Eliza. How lonesome both of them must have been.

She'd been lonely in her relationship with Brandon.

Even when they were together in the same place, he hadn't really been with her, not fully. Something else usually occupied his attention. He was always either looking at his phone, watching television, or else his gaze had been constantly in motion, as if looking for someone more interesting than her.

"But it's going to change." Charles gave a decisive nod. "Things will be different when I go back to my time."

Megan only offered him an encouraging smile. Her excitement for the night's activities dimmed, however, to hear him talk about returning to his era. In a short time, he'd become her friend. And now… she had begun to want more than just friendship.

There was no point in developing feelings for Charles, not when he was so determined to return to 1902—and Eliza.

But Megan's foolish heart wasn't listening to her. She was headed straight for heartbreak despite all her logical reasoning.

At some point, he was going to leave. On top of which, he was far too much of a gentleman to turn his attention to anyone other than his fiancée.

Megan wouldn't stand in the way of that.

Behind her, the mayor started to give a short speech, but Megan wasn't listening.

"Want to take a selfie?" she asked suddenly. If, or when, he did return to 1902, she wanted something to remember him by.

"A what-ie?" He looked baffled.

"It's a self-portrait. Here." She pulled out her phone and stood close to him. It was hard to stay focused with him so near, smelling of cool December air and pine, but she told herself, *We're just friends.* She held out her arm. "Okay, on the count of three, say 'Christmas!'"

He frowned for a moment, then edged even closer to her. His skin had a nice scent, too. *Oh, boy. Help.*

"One. Two. Three. Christmas!"

"Christmas," Charles said brightly.

The tree's lights burst to life behind them, just as the flash on her phone went off. Everyone applauded and said, *Ooh* and *Aah!* It *was* a spectacular sight, blazing with hundreds of colorful lights. The carolers launched into a chorus of "O Christmas Tree," and the crowd joined in. Not everybody had the best singing voices, but what was lacking in ability was made up for in enthusiasm.

For Megan's own preservation, she put a little space between her and Charles before looking down at the screen to see how the picture turned out. But Charles stood close beside her as he, too, checked out the photo.

In the picture, she and Charles had their heads close together, and they both wore big smiles. The tree made for an enchanting backdrop, filling the space behind them with light and color.

"We look pretty darned adorable," she said, trying to focus on the photo.

"I cannot believe that your telephone also serves as

a camera. But yes, we do look 'pretty darned adorable,' if I may say so."

"You may." She might even turn it into her phone's wallpaper.

"Megan! Honey!"

She turned, then whooped with happiness as she saw a quartet of very dear, very familiar faces approaching.

"You know those people?" Charles asked in a whisper.

"I should hope so." She waved her arm over her head. "They're my family."

CHAPTER NINE

Charles walked warily behind Megan as she eagerly hurried to her family.

Families were tricky things—he'd lost his, and though Eliza had tried to bring him into hers, he could never quite feel at home with them. For one thing, though his parents had been hardworking people, with his father employed as a pharmacist and his mother assisting behind the counter, they'd never had much money.

Eliza's parents were part of New York's elite, the Four Hundred. They had been kind to Charles, never snobbish, but he couldn't feel comfortable with them. Or perhaps...he didn't let himself feel comfortable with them. He often left their dinners early in order to attend to business, and routinely but politely declined their offers to have him stay with them at their summer home in the Hamptons.

He'd also planned to turn down Eliza's invitation to have him celebrate Christmas with her family.

Perhaps he ought to make excuses to Megan and return home. He could find a ride…somehow…and keep himself from meeting the Turners. After all, he wasn't intending to stay in the twenty-first century. Why take the time to get to know them?

"Charles," Megan said, turning to him and beckoning him forward with a smile. "I want you to meet them. I promise they won't make you sing Christmas carols," she added and laughed. "Not today, anyway."

He found himself hurrying to catch up with her. Four eager faces looked at him with open curiosity.

"I'm so glad we ran into you," Megan said, beaming at her family. They were all dressed in festive sweaters and thick woolen coats. "There's someone I want you guys to meet. Charles, this is my mom, Sharon, and my dad, Greg."

She gestured to a handsome woman with dark curly hair that was very like Megan's, and to a man with graying hair and spectacles who had trimmed his wheelchair with tinsel garlands.

"Mr. and Mrs. Turner," Charles said, shaking their hands.

"Please, call us Greg and Sharon," Megan's mother said at once.

"This handsome guy is my brother, Nathan," Megan continued, nodding at a very fit-looking man who bore a particular resemblance to her. "And this beautiful lady with him is his wife, Elena."

Charles shook hands with Megan's brother and sister-in-law. "A pleasure."

"Megan, honey," Greg said. "Who's your friend?"

Though Megan's cheeks were pink from the cold, they turned even brighter pink. "Right. This is the mansion's new reenactor for Charles Whitley."

"I'm Charles," he said.

"That's funny," Nathan said, "having the same name as the guy you play."

"It is, rather."

For the time he had remaining in this era, Charles had to tread carefully. Having a handful of people know about his time traveling was all right, but if more people knew, they might start asking questions and putting both him and Megan in some uncomfortable situations. There was always the possibility that they'd deem him mad and lock him away in an asylum. Things could snowball easily.

"Is this your first tree lighting in Cutter Springs?" Elena asked.

"Yes, and it's quite the spectacle."

Much as he disliked admitting to it, there was something delightful about joining together with the community to welcome in the holiday. The tree lighting gave him a sense of belonging and warmth.

"My family's from south Texas," Elena said cheerfully, "so it took me a while to get used to the whole Christmas-with-snow thing."

"I'm navigating the holiday, myself," Charles answered.

"Charles," Sharon said, turning to him. "What are you doing tomorrow night?"

"Most likely, watching the television," he admitted.

"Not anymore," Megan's mother said. "You're coming to our family's Christmas party."

"Yeah!" Nathan said with enthusiasm. "You should come. It's tradition!"

"Oh…well…that's very…." He shifted uncomfortably.

Run! part of him shouted.

Stay! another cried. *I could learn about holiday family traditions.*

It was safer to go through life without forming bonds with people, avoiding hurt in case they disappeared or were lost. Everyone could be put in neat boxes, no one touching him. He'd never have to face the pain he had experienced when his parents had died.

Stifling a sense of anxiety, he glanced at Megan.

She sidled close to him. "This is exactly what you need," she whispered. "Family, and the Christmas spirit."

"I'm not certain it's a good idea."

"Dan, Lydia, and Sophia are going to be there. You'll be among friends."

He exhaled, still uncertain. Looking at Megan's sparkling eyes and seeing her encouraging smile, however, something within him unknotted.

He'd be leaving soon. No need to concern himself with forming attachments.

And…she'd be there.

"All right," he said finally. "I'll come to the party."

Her smile melted the last vestiges of his unease. "Before we go to the party, are you up for a little theater? Amber can hold some seats for us at the Christmas one-acts show, and after, we'll go to my parents'."

A holiday theatrical performance *and* a Christmas party? Did he dare immerse himself so deeply in the spirit of the season?

"That sounds delightful," he said.

"That's great! I'll pick you up at six, and just have a light snack. Nobody leaves a Turner Christmas party with an empty stomach."

"I am looking forward to it," he said, and surprised himself with the genuine enthusiasm in his voice.

It was becoming clear that if Megan asked him to do something, he was all too eager to agree.

It was silly to spend so long getting ready for the theater and her family's Christmas party. At the theater, she'd be in the dark, and for the party, Megan knew everyone there. She'd known most of them for years. It wasn't like she had to get super spiffy.

And yet, here she was, staring into her closet for a solid thirty minutes, debating what she wanted to wear. The velvet dress? Too fancy. The T-shirt that read, *I Just Want to Decorate Christmas Trees and Eat Peppermint Bark*? Not fancy enough.

Finally, she settled on a dark floral top and some winter white jeans, which she paired with ankle boots and the pearl earrings her parents had given her when she'd gotten her PhD.

Megan eyed her laptop, reflected behind her in the mirror. She really ought to email Professor Coyle and ask about her letter of recommendation. The teaching job wasn't going to just show up at her door. But every time she sat down and opened a blank email page, she gave up and surfed interesting American history websites instead.

"Ugh," she said aloud. "Either do it or don't, but stop torturing yourself."

Yet she didn't go to her computer, and she didn't put it from her mind. It stuck there like a lump of unmelted cocoa in the bottom of her mug.

At least thinking about the letter of recommendation briefly took her mind off of fretting about her appearance tonight.

She spent extra time doing her makeup, though, making sure it didn't look too heavy or not heavy enough. The last time she'd taken so much care with her cosmetics, she'd been prepping for the prom.

Why am I doing this?

It had *nothing* to do with Charles being her friend-date tonight. Nothing at all.

Keep telling yourself that.

After the hurtful breakup with Brandon, she wasn't eager to get back into the dating world. Though the internet opened up a world of possibilities for meeting people with similar interests, folks who geeked out about nineteenth-and-twentieth-century American history weren't all that common. It wasn't as though putting "tour guide, living history reenactor, and wannabe history professor" on an online dating profile would net her tons of hits from interested guys.

It was all theoretical, anyway. She didn't have the guts to get the letter from Professor Coyle, and she certainly didn't want to face the lack of interest from men on a dating app.

Alone at Christmas. Again.

With a groan of frustration, she wheeled away from the mirror and grabbed her coat, hat, and scarf. Moments later, she was out the door, heading to the mansion.

Her heart gave a ridiculous leap when she saw Charles waiting for her outside. Though his clothes were borrowed from Nathan, Charles looked exceptionally handsome, as though everything had been purchased just for him. His midnight-blue V-neck sweater was nicely complemented by his brown corduroy pants, and his hunter-green scarf was tied around his neck with a dash of panache.

As he climbed into the car and fastened his seatbelt, she said, "You look very nice."

"And you look quite pretty," he said, and then went red. "I mean, what you're wearing is exceptionally attractive. That is, you always look attractive but "

"That's okay," she said, patting his hand and feeling charmed by both his compliments and his discombobulation. "I know what you meant. Ready to get a little culture and then stuff yourself with Christmas cookies?"

"I await the artistic spectacle." He patted his flat

stomach. "And there's plenty of room in here for every variety of holiday treats."

She chuckled and drove toward the theater. "You can pick a radio station."

"A world of music right at your fingertips," he said, fiddling with the tuner knob. He winced when a loud pop station came on with its jangly instrumentation and insistent vocals. "Is this what passes for music nowadays? It sounds like a calliope colliding with a candy factory."

Megan laughed at the apt description. "Fortunately, there are enough stations for everyone's taste. Maybe you'd like this."

She pressed a button and classical music swirled in the interior of the car.

"Very nice," he said with a nod, "but don't forget, I'm still a man of the people. This sort of music makes me think of interminable dinner parties. Perhaps we can find some ragtime. That's very modern. Or, it was."

"Not so common, anymore," she said with an apologetic smile. "Want to keep looking?"

He turned the knob, and when the Christmas station came on, his hand hovered but didn't change the station. She smiled to herself when he sat back, letting the holiday music fill the car.

"So," he said, "tell me, Miss Megan Turner, how fares your quest for getting that letter of recommendation?"

Wow, it was like he'd been in her head. Which was kind of weird, but also kind of nice.

"It's so busy at work, and the holiday, and…" She stopped. Even she couldn't quite believe her excuses.

"May I remind you," he said, "that Rosie, my housekeeper, got whatever she wanted. A force of nature, that Rosie."

"It sounds like it!"

"I hired her on the spot when she applied for the position, even though she had next to no experience. But she just marched into my study and said, 'Mr. Whitley, *you need me.*' I was convinced."

"Wow," Megan said. "That took some serious courage on her part."

"It did, and I doubt you could play her so believably if you didn't have that strength in yourself."

She absorbed his words. Was it true? Was she really as gutsy as Rosie? She'd always believed she was timid. She didn't speak up when people cut in front of her in line, and she never took the last slice of cake. Yet maybe there was a kernel of truth in what Charles said.

No—she was nice, quiet Megan, not plucky, outspoken Rosie. Even Brandon thought she was a boring little mouse, stuck in her books, stuck in the past.

"What should I do?" she asked. "Just show up at Professor Coyle's office and demand the letter?"

"That is *exactly* what I think you should do."

"It's not that easy," she said, her voice heavy with doubt.

"When I developed my idea for improving the milling process, I knew that if I didn't present it to the mill's owner, it would never be put into use and never become patented. I could have made excuses, or talked myself out of going to his office with my idea. But I understood that I had to make an opportunity for myself." He sent her a meaningful look. "No one is going to give you a teaching position. You have to go out and get what you want. And I *know* you're capable. So...take the chance."

Megan chewed this over as they finished the rest of the drive in silence. Charles had so much faith in her, but did she have faith in herself? She just didn't know, and that doubt made her doubt herself all over again.

She put this uncertainty from her mind as they reached the theater. It was a small performance space, with just ninety-nine seats to meet with the actors' union regulations. After she and Charles collected their tickets, they milled around the lobby.

The space was full of people excitedly buzzing in anticipation of the show, including a few folks holding bouquets of flowers for the actors. Posters for past and upcoming productions lined the walls, and some preshow Christmas music played softly on the sound system.

"Occasionally," Charles said as they waited to be escorted into the theater itself, "Eliza would try encouraging me to accompany her to the theater in New York. There was an actress, Mrs. Fiske, who had been taking the theatrical scene by storm."

"I've heard of her! She was supposed to be amazing. But...I'm hearing the *would try* in that sentence."

He smiled ruefully. "Eliza wasn't successful. There was always too much to do rather than waste my time, sitting in the dark, watching people pretend to be something they weren't."

Megan tilted her head as she regarded him. "Does that mean you've never been to the theater?"

"This will be my first time at an actual theatrical performance," he admitted.

A teenager dressed like an elf handed them programs, while an usher asked, "Can I escort you to your seats?"

Megan showed her their tickets, and the usher guided them to the seats that were excellently placed right in the middle, not too close to the stage, and not too far.

After thanking the usher, Megan and Charles took their seats. Within the theater itself, the eagerness for the performance was even higher, judging by the happy chatter of the audience. She was happy to see that there were children in the crowd, a few of them bouncing in their chairs. It was good to get kids exposed to the arts early.

Which reminded her... "I hope you're looking forward to seeing your very first play," she said to Charles.

"I rather am," he said, sounding surprised by his own anticipation. "But I'll need you to advise me about proper theater etiquette. I don't want to do anything crass or gauche, like blow my nose right in the middle of an important soliloquy."

Megan laughed. "If you know that, you're already ahead of the game. I should tell you that it's rude to talk during a performance, and also you should silence your phone or turn it off altogether." She quickly hit the mute button on her phone.

He did so, too, though he mumbled under his breath, "No one telephones me, anyway."

"I'll call you. Whenever you want." Only after the words left her mouth did she realize what they meant. So she quickly added, "Except during the show. And, um, first thing in the morning. I can't really verbalize before I have my latte."

You're babbling.

She pressed her lips together to keep from spewing more nonsense.

Fortunately, Charles didn't seem to have noticed her chatter. He looked around the theater, taking everything in, from the illuminated EXIT signs to the upright piano at the foot of the stage.

Megan thumbed through the program, and noted that three one-act plays were going to be performed that night, all of them with holiday themes. The first play was called "Eight Nights of Fun," and looked to be about Hanukkah, followed by a piece titled, "A Kwanzaa Harvest For Kayla." The final play was "The Christmas Caper," and Megan recognized the name of the playwright as the head of the university theater department.

Amber would be appearing in all three plays.

The lights began to dim, causing the audience to

clap, and Charles whispered to her with undisguised excitement, "I think it's starting!"

She tapped her finger to her lips, gently reminding him to be quiet, and he gave her a bashful grin in response.

The curtain rose—and magic happened. For the next hour and a half, Megan found herself transported from the little theater in Cutter Springs to places across the country, from a Chicago suburb, to bustling Atlanta, and finally, to a rural town very much like this one. She laughed at the silly antics and teared up when the characters had touching moments, especially those that involved family.

Occasionally, she glanced at Charles and smiled to see how engrossed he was in the performance. His gaze never left the stage, and he gasped aloud at surprising reveals or laughed from deep in his belly at particularly funny lines.

And whenever Amber appeared onstage, no one could look away. The fussiest, most restless children quieted down. She was riveting, conveying genuine emotion without being melodramatic. Megan noticed that even the ushers' eyes were glued to Amber whenever she was on the stage, despite the fact that they had been present for every performance.

"She's extraordinary," Charles whispered.

Megan nodded, a sense of pride suffusing her. It wasn't the first time Megan had seen Amber act, but she got better and better every time.

When the curtain fell on the final play, the audience

surged to its feet, applauding loudly. The cast emerged to take their group bows. There was no mistaking the joy in Amber's beaming face. Clearly, she loved acting, and it was easy to get swept up in her enthusiasm for her craft.

The cast eventually left the stage and the audience filed out.

"Let's wait in the lobby for Amber," Megan said as they walked toward the rear of the theater.

Charles nodded in agreement. "Such a performance ought to be commended."

It wasn't long before the cast emerged, dressed in their everyday clothing. Friends and family surrounded the actors, accompanied by many hugs and photos.

When Amber appeared, wearing a shy smile, Megan immediately came forward and hugged her tightly.

"Oh my goodness," Megan exclaimed. "That was *amazing*."

"Was it really okay?" Amber looked back and forth between Megan and Charles.

"Let there be no doubt that your performance was sublime," Charles said. "Had I known that theater could be so extraordinary, I would have attended long ago. Yet I am certain that I would not have been half so captivated were it not for the depth you brought to your roles."

Pink tinted Amber's cheeks. "You guys."

"Amber," Megan said, taking hold of her friend's hand, "you *have* to audition for that Broadway play. Before you say no," she added hurriedly when it looked like Amber was going to protest, "just think about this—more people should be seeing your work and your talent. It's something that needs to be shared with the world."

"I agree," Charles said.

Megan burned with the need to have everyone recognize how incredible Amber was as an actor. She'd been completely truthful in telling Amber that the world needed to see her talent. Her potential was on the verge of being fully realized. All she needed was to take the next step.

"I'm just not sure." Amber twisted her hands together. "It's one thing to audition for shows around here, but putting myself out there for a Broadway production? That's a really big deal. I mean, I haven't done *any* theater in Manhattan."

"It is a big deal," Megan said. "And that's exactly why you should go for it. I'll even help you put an audition video together. Just think about it." She gave Amber another hug. "Are you going to come to my parents' Christmas party?"

"I'm going to my aunt's to watch *Scrooged*. It's kind of a tradition." Amber smiled at Megan and Charles, her eyes brimming with emotion. "Thanks for coming. It means a lot."

"The honor was entirely ours." Charles bowed.

"Speaking of the party," Megan said, consulting her watch, "we'd better go. See you tomorrow at work."

Amber waved goodbye just as fellow cast members encircled her to commend her performance.

"Ready for a party?" Megan asked Charles as they walked outside.

"My first visit to a theater," he said, "and my first Christmas party."

"A night of firsts."

Fifteen minutes later, Megan and Charles pulled up outside her parents' house. The front was adorned with lights and ornaments, and several tasteful reindeer statues stood in the snow-covered front yard. Even the wheelchair ramp was festooned with red and green garlands.

She smiled, as she always did whenever she saw her parents' Christmas decorations.

"I take it this is your parents' home," Charles said drily.

"What gave it away?" she said, struggling to keep her face straight.

"Other than the fact that it says *The Turners* on your post box, they clearly share your love of the holiday. It's the brightest house on the block." His expression turned thoughtful. "Though my parents didn't have much, they always made certain I had an orange and a new toy in my Christmas stocking." He exhaled. "I'd forgotten about that—until now."

"Hey," she said with sympathy, "if spending time with someone else's family makes you uncomfortable, we can go. It's really all right."

He smiled, though it looked a little strained. "Your family was kind enough to extend an invitation to me, so I won't be a churl and refuse."

"'Churl.' What an old-fashioned word."

"It means—"

"I know what it means!" She grinned at him. Brandon used to tease her for using what he called "old-timey" words, but she didn't have to worry about that with Charles. "I just like hearing you say it. But seriously, my folks will completely understand if you're not up for this. They won't think you're being churlish."

"I've set my mind to truly experiencing Christmas," he said, slapping his palms on his thighs, "And once I set my mind to something, I do it."

Her heart warmed at his determination. Hard not to admire someone who deliberately picked a difficult path because they knew it would be a challenge.

You could learn something there.

"Then prepare yourself," she said, unfastening her seatbelt. "You're about to experience a Turner Family Christmas."

CHAPTER TEN

Charles braced himself as he climbed the steps to the Turners' home. He wasn't entirely certain what it was he was bracing himself for, but it was a challenge not to put up the instinctive protective barriers he'd carried with him for nearly eighteen years.

Even so, those barriers wobbled when presented with Megan's generous heart and her genuine love of the season. Would it be the same with her family, or would he feel pushed further away?

She gave him a wink as she knocked on the front door. His stuttering pulse calmed, and he found himself winking back. He never winked! And yet, here he was, performing the silly but charming gesture.

The door opened, and Charles found himself presented with the spectacle of Greg and Sharon Turner wearing gaily-patterned sweaters and two of the most absurd hats he'd ever seen. Greg's was a woman's enormous sun hat, complete with gigantic silk flowers, while Sharon wore a rubber bathing cap that buckled beneath her chin.

"Merry Christmas!" the Turners cried in unison.

Before either Megan or Charles could speak, they thrust a hat into their daughter's hands and one into Charles's.

He held it out for inspection. It looked to be a Renaissance-era courtier's cap, complete with an extravagant feather plume.

"Oh, I didn't mention," Megan said, setting a red firefighter's helmet on her head. "It's a Turner tradition to wear a silly hat at our Christmas party."

"This certainly *is* silly." He tapped the feather on his cap, making it bob.

"Nobody sets foot inside without putting on a hat," Greg said cheerfully.

Charles drew in a breath.

To heck with it. Dignity is overrated, anyway.

He set the hat on his head, and Sharon clapped.

"Perfect!" Megan's mother said. "You look like a poet, ready to compose a verse in praise of your lady fair."

Charles's gaze immediately went to Megan, who was too busy fussing with her father's floppy hat to notice. Just as quickly as he looked at her, Charles glanced away.

What was that about?

Megan was *not* his lady fair. She'd been nothing but kind to him, and he wouldn't repay that kindness with unwanted feelings. And there was Eliza to consider.

He had to return to her, to the future they were meant to have together.

But he caught Sharon gazing at him with speculation, as if he'd given away an important secret.

"Now that you're suitably attired," Greg announced, "come on in."

Charles trailed after Megan as she stepped into the house. She hadn't gone very far before she was embraced by her brother—wearing what appeared to be a multicolored cap topped with a propeller—and her brother's wife, who wore a bright yellow helmet of unknown design.

"Glad you could make it to the madness," Nathan said to Charles when he released his sister from their hug.

"I wouldn't dream of missing it," Charles said—and he wasn't lying.

Within minutes of being amidst the Turners, he felt welcome and comfortable. Whether that was their doing alone, or in some way Megan's accomplishment, he wasn't certain.

There were other people gathered in the home, everyone in absurd hats, but he spotted Dan, Lydia, and Sophia standing in front of the fireplace. The Romano family waved at him, and he waved back.

He glanced around the house. It was both open and snug, full of warm wood and cozy fabric. There was nothing imposing about it. No one was trying to impress anyone. It simply existed as a space where people could gather and be happy. He imagined that

Megan and Nathan had both enjoyed safe, loving childhoods here in this secure and relaxed house.

His home—he refused to think of it as the Whitley-*Moran* Mansion—had been designed to be beautiful and stately, more a testament to what he'd been able to build for himself rather than a place where good memories could be made. When Charles returned to his era, he'd take a page from the Turners' book and soften up his house's hard edges. Perhaps bring in furniture that was more comfortable and less stately. Surely that would please Megan—*Eliza*.

He shook his head at himself.

"Have a cookie," Sharon said, holding up a tray. "There's cocoa in the kitchen, too."

"Both are must-haves at the Turner Christmas party," Megan said. She plucked a frosted cookie from the tray and took a healthy bite.

Charles took a cookie and bit into it. At once, the flavors of butter, lemon, and ginger filled his mouth. It was all he could do to keep from greedily stuffing the whole thing into his mouth.

"This is delicious," he said solemnly. "Sharon, I must have the recipe for my—" He stopped himself before he admitted he had a cook. Or rather, that he'd had one in 1902. Right now, he was learning the capabilities of a microwave oven. "For myself."

Megan pointed at her father. "*He's* the baker."

"Got the social media presence to show for it," Nathan added.

"Is that like a newspaper?" Charles asked.

"Here." Greg pulled out one of the phones no one in this era could live without, poked at for a moment, and then held it up for Charles's inspection. "This is from my Pinterest board."

Beautiful images of different baked goods appeared on the screen. There were cookies, cakes, breads, and pastries, all artfully lit and displayed.

"My gracious," Charles said on a breath. "This is incredible. And you did all of it?"

"Well," Greg said, flushing with pride, "Sharon helps me set the lights up, but the baking and styling, that's all me."

"How perfectly marvelous," Charles said sincerely. "And people share their photographs on this... Pinterest?"

"You've never heard of Pinterest?" Elena asked, tilting her head in curiosity.

Charles's mind went blank. He had no idea how to answer Elena's question. *Actually, I've traveled over a hundred years into the future, so I'm a little behind on technological developments.*

"Charles has been working abroad for the past few years," Megan said quickly.

Everyone nodded, accepting her explanation. Charles exhaled in relief.

Little Sophia—wearing what looked like a knight's helmet, except stitched from soft, silver fabric—appeared beside Megan.

"Come roast marshmallows with me," she demanded, brandishing a pointed stick.

"My knight has commanded me," Megan said, and laughed as she followed Sophia to the fireplace where Dan and Lydia were in the process of setting marshmallows on fire.

Charles watched as Megan helped the little girl spear a marshmallow on a long skewer. Both Megan and Sophia looked very studious, with Megan appearing to speak in a very patient and kind manner. He had a glimpse of Megan as an academic. If she taught with the same focus and attention as she helped Sophia roast marshmallows, surely she must be an incredible teacher. The university would be lucky to have her.

Anyone would be lucky to have her.

He started when someone clasped him in a tight embrace.

"It's so good to meet you, Charles," Sharon said, then stepped back to release him. "I like you so much more than Brandon."

"Who is Brandon?"

Sharon grimaced. "Oh. You didn't know about him?"

"No. I think I can guess, however." This Brandon person must be Megan's suitor.

The room suddenly felt too warm, and Charles fought the impulse to grind his teeth.

Am I jealous?

But it couldn't be. Charles was surely not jealous of whoever chose to court Megan. She had a perfect right to spend time with anyone she liked. And he was returning to his own era, hopefully soon. He couldn't claim any part of her life.

You're engaged to Eliza, as well. Don't forget about that.

Both Megan and Eliza deserved better. True, without him in her life, Eliza would go on to marry Harold Moran—the thought still made Charles shudder. But they'd raised a family, one that had prospered and thrived for generations. Eliza had recovered from losing him. But even so, Charles had promised himself to her. She needed someone who honored a commitment. He took his commitments seriously. He had to do better by her, and upon his return, he would.

"Brandon's not in the picture anymore," Nathan said, breaking into Charles's thoughts.

"Oh. I see." The invisible, tight band that had wrapped around Charles suddenly disappeared. The notion was simultaneously comforting and alarming. "That's…that's fine."

"Sure, dude." Nathan gave him a sly grin.

Heavens, was Charles as transparent as that? He helped himself to another cookie rather than face the answer to that question.

Megan poured herself a cup of cocoa. She looked out the window over the kitchen sink and saw Charles standing alone on the back porch, watching the snow fall.

She winced. No doubt he wanted to get away from

the madness inside the house. Had it been a mistake to drag him into the middle of her family's boisterous holiday tradition? He'd been pretty set against celebrating Christmas.

Or maybe he just wanted a little bit of air. Between the roaring fire and press of people, the atmosphere in the house might be a little close.

Only one way to find out.

She poured a second mug of cocoa, dropped a few marshmallows into it, and carried the cups out to the back porch.

"Hey there," she said, stepping outside. Cool air immediately stung her face, but she welcomed the sensation after the warmth inside. "Brought you some cocoa."

Charles turned at her approach. To her relief, he greeted her arrival with a smile.

"Thank you." He took the mug from her and sipped. "I taste a bit of cinnamon. Your father's recipe?"

"We've made adjustments to it over the years. The cinnamon was Elena's addition." She also sipped at her drink, letting the spice and chocolate coat her tongue.

"Just like the cookies, the cocoa is delicious."

"Traditions get better when they grow and adapt over the years."

He was silent for a moment. "You're quite fortunate, you know. To have your family so close."

She nodded.

"I do know it. Whenever a holiday or birthday rolls around, I'm reminded again of how lucky I am."

She considered him over the rim of her mug. "Is that why you don't care for Christmas? Because you lost your parents?"

After another drink of cocoa, he set his mug down. "I didn't used to think so. I believed that I was too busy and focused on work to waste valuable time on sentiment."

"Something changed."

He glanced toward the house, where the sounds of laughter and music could be heard. His expression was pensive, and she wondered how much thought he'd given this.

"I held back," he said softly.

"Why?"

"I think it was my fear of getting attached to anyone, or forming true, lasting connections."

She contemplated this. "Because if you got attached and something happened, it would hurt all the more."

"Just as it had when I lost my parents." His gaze was warm as he looked at her. "You're quite perceptive, Miss Megan Turner."

His praise made her cheeks hot, and she glanced down.

"I have my moments," she said dismissively.

"A little egotism is healthy. It keeps us moving forward, and gives us room to dream." The corners of his eyes crinkled. "Again, you're too unwilling to recognize your own abilities."

Megan swallowed. He had a way of seeing right into the core of her, and she suddenly understood his fear of letting someone get too close. There would come a time when Charles returned to his time. If she allowed herself to get close to him, if she came to think of him as a friend—as more than a friend—his leaving would cut a hole out of her.

Anyway, she wasn't nearly the courageous, insightful person he seemed to think she was. She was just ordinary Megan. Someone who loved teaching people about history but couldn't summon the backbone to ask a professor for a letter of recommendation.

But she didn't want to talk about herself or whether she recognized her own strength. This time was about Charles.

"There's one thing I definitely know I'm good at," she said, lifting the lid on a wooden storage locker. "Hula Hoop!"

She held up two plastic hoops, one red and one green.

"What...are...those?" Charles asked with a perplexed frown. He took the hoop she offered him and shook it, making it rattle.

She walked down the steps of the porch onto the snow-covered back lawn, with Charles following. Snow drifted down and dusted their hair.

"Hoop toys have been around in different cultures since forever," she said, stepping into the hoop. "But Richard Knerr and Arthur Melin created a plastic version in 1958, and trademarked the name 'Hula Hoop.' It was a huge craze back in the '50s, but people still love it today. And," she added with a grin, "I always beat Nathan whenever we had Hula-Hooping contests."

Charles lifted an eyebrow.

She blushed. "Okay, I'm getting into full-on history geek mode, but I can't help it! There's so much history behind everything."

"And how does one 'Hula-Hoop?'" He studied the toy as if he could somehow motorize it and make it five times as profitable.

But Hula-Hooping wasn't about profit—it was strictly for fun.

"Watch and learn from the master."

She spun the hoop around her waist and began to twist. It had been a while, but she quickly got her rhythm back, and within moments, the hoop spun around her. The feel of the spinning plastic hoop brought her right back to childhood, when she and Nathan would challenge each other for nothing more than bragging rights. Mom used to watch, and afterwards they'd go for milkshakes.

Charles gaped at her.

"That looks impossible!" he exclaimed.

"Try it," she said. "Here, I'll show you." She demonstrated the movements to get the hoop moving and how to keep it up. "Like that. See?"

His expression skeptical, he tried to get the hoop going around his waist. It immediately fell to the snow. He tried again, and again, muttering to himself all the while. Finally, on his fourth attempt, he managed to get it to spin around his waist.

"I did it!" He beamed.

She chuckled. "You're good at everything."

"Not so. I simply don't give up." He eyed her. "Ready for a drubbing, Miss Turner?"

She made herself look as steely and fierce as possible. "Bring it on."

"I'm not certain what that means," he said, narrowing his eyes, "but if it's a challenge you're after, it's a challenge you're going to get."

As the snow fell, and the sounds of holiday merriment floated over the backyard, and the lights along the porch twinkled, Megan and Charles Hula-Hooped, laughing and taunting each other. Her sides hurt and her cheeks ached from smiling, but she couldn't make herself stop. It was Christmas, she was having fun, and she was sharing a moment with a guy who appreciated her.

It was perfect.

Her smile faded as she realized that everything was too perfect. Because it couldn't last.

CHAPTER ELEVEN

Even though she'd already eaten close to a dozen cookies, Megan couldn't stop herself as she wandered into the kitchen in search of more. She might regret it later, and would have to run an extra lap around the neighborhood tomorrow so she could squeeze into her jeans, but for now, she'd simply wallow in the joy that was her dad's Lemon Ginger Shortbread with Rum Glaze.

"Oh, I know," her mom said as she stood on the other side of the kitchen island. "I think there must be some kind of elf-dust in those things that make me eat them by the handful."

"Cookies today," Megan said, "kale tomorrow."

"Maybe I can convince your dad to make kale cookies."

Megan tilted her head in thought. "I can't decide if that sounds delicious or awful."

"A little of both." Her mother nibbled a cookie before saying abruptly, "I like Charles."

"Me, too," Megan said. Then, "Maybe a little more than I should."

It felt strange to say it aloud, to admit to herself that she was developing feelings for Charles, but if there was anyone she could trust, it was Mom. She'd been there when, in the sixth grade, Megan had cried into her pillow while confessing her unrequited crush on a boy in class. After that, they'd gone into the living room and watched a cartoon marathon.

Mom had been there when Megan had called home from college in tears after the breakup with Zane from down the hall of the dormitory—even though it had been a mutual and friendly split. A couple days after that phone call, Megan had received a care package containing her beloved stuffed raccoon toy and a tin of double chocolate cookies, plus a few gossip magazines, just because.

Mom just knew what Megan needed.

Her mom's eyes were thoughtful as she asked, "Why do you say that?"

"Because..." Megan sighed. "He's going to go home, and there's someone waiting for him." It hurt to say it aloud, but she needed to come to terms with reality. He had made it plain that he was going back to ensure that he, and not Harold Moran, married Eliza. Maybe he hadn't professed his undying love for his fiancée, but he wouldn't marry her unless he cared.

"Oh," Mom said sadly.

"Yeah. I mean, it's okay. It's fine." Hopefully, the

more she said things like that, the more she'd believe it. "He sees me as just a friend, anyway."

"Really?" Mom tilted her head in a gesture that showed she didn't quite agree. "I don't know about that. I've seen the way he looks at you, and there's a lot more than friendship in his eyes."

Heat crept up into Megan's face.

"You're being ridiculous," she said with a wave of her hand.

"I may have dressed up like a warty witch for Halloween," Mom said, "so I know how to be ridiculous. One thing I'd never joke about, though, is my children's happiness."

Megan shook her head, but her gaze moved past her mother and into the living room, where Charles, Elena, and Dan were deep in conversation. Elena was showing Charles her phone.

"I can show you how to set up a playlist," Elena said enthusiastically.

"Any music I want," Charles murmured, "whenever I want it?"

"Wait until you hear what's possible," Dan said with a grin.

At that moment, Charles looked up at Megan. Their gazes locked and held.

A thrill traveled from the top of her head to the tips of her fingers and toes. When he smiled, she thought she'd melt into a puddle right there on the kitchen floor.

"I rest my case," Mom said, but Megan barely heard

her. Her mind spun with the possibility that maybe, just maybe, Charles thought of her as more than his Twenty-First-Century Holiday Tour Guide.

Could she dare to hope?

Charles's heart lodged in his throat as he and Megan looked at each other. His mind kept returning to their conversation on the porch, and what it had meant to let someone inside. He'd always just barreled ahead, focusing on what he could achieve instead of considering the needs of his heart.

But there was something magical about Hula-Hooping in the snow. It was frivolous and juvenile and also wonderful—even more so because it was a shared experience.

Megan had given him that.

She'd taken him to the theater, as well. They'd sat in the dark with a bunch of strangers, all of them sharing the same emotions. He'd dismissed theatrics as trivial and nonessential, but he'd been quite wrong. He'd felt things that transported him from joy to sadness and back to joy again.

Megan had given him that, too.

"Mr. Whitley."

He felt a tug on his arm and looked down to see Sophia standing beside him. Along with her knight's helmet, she wore a dejected expression. At once, he crouched down so their faces were level.

"What's wrong, Sophia?"

"I've looked and I've looked." She heaved a deep sigh. "But I can't find anything in your journal that could help you go back to your time."

He quickly glanced around to make sure that no one was nearby who might overhear their conversation.

"You're certain?" he asked, once he was confident nobody was listening.

"There are lots of cool ideas for inventions and stuff," Sophia said. "The last thing you wrote was about was getting that clock in Paris. But that's it. I'm really sorry."

Her small face furrowed with a scowl, but her anger was directed at herself, which Charles would not permit.

"Nothing to be sorry about," he said at once. "I'll wager that even the brainiest scientist would have a deuce of a time figuring out this problem."

"But how will you get home?" she asked sadly.

It stunned him to realize that he hadn't been giving the matter much thought. He'd been enjoying his work at the mansion too much. And the time he'd spent with Megan, enjoying the holiday, had been utterly delightful.

Getting back needed to be his prime motivation. He had to return and triumph over Moran. Yet life in this era became more and more appealing the longer he was here.

He had a sinking realization as to why that might be.

"I am certain that we'll think of something. In the

meantime," he added thoughtfully, "being in this era isn't so bad."

"I guess so." Yet the girl didn't sound convinced.

"I know so. There are things like playlists and cars that run on electricity and education for everyone and—"

"And friends!" Sophia said cheerfully. "Like me and my dad and Megan."

"Precisely."

He couldn't keep himself from looking over at Megan as she and her brother laughed while trading hats. There was such animation in her face, such openness and pleasure in living life and having experiences.

No one would fault him for admiring those aspects of her. That's all it was, wasn't it? Simply a matter of appreciating admirable qualities in someone?

It took some effort to look away from her, but he managed to do so.

"I think I heard that there are still some ornaments left to be put on the tree," he said to Sophia. "Would you care to join me in decorating the tree?"

"Yes!" She barely let him finish his sentence, taking his hand and dragging him toward the tree.

He told himself that he *would* take pleasure in the moment, because everything else was uncertain.

By the time the very last cookie had been eaten, and a number of "selfies" had been taken, it was quite late.

Sophia slept in her father's arms, her head on Dan's shoulder, as the Romanos bid their farewells. The rest of the guests filtered out the door, leaving behind the Turners and Charles.

Megan emerged from a closet, holding her and Charles's coats.

"You can't leave now," Greg protested.

"What about an eggnog-drinking contest?" Nathan said.

"Good gracious," Charles muttered under his breath. He couldn't imagine anyone drinking eggnog quickly, let alone in volume.

"Sorry, guys," she said, handing Charles his overcoat, "but tomorrow's a work day, and—oh, thanks." She aimed a smile at Charles as he held her coat, then slipped her arms into the sleeves.

"Such a gentleman," Sharon said approvingly.

My goodness, this era had to be starved for manners to consider holding a lady's coat to be commendable. Still, it felt quite nice to perform the simple task for Megan, and to catch the faint whiff of wood smoke and perfume in her hair.

"Mr. and Mrs. Turner," he said, turning to the couple.

Greg held up his hand. "Nuh-uh."

"Greg, Sharon," Charles said instead. "Thank you for your hospitality."

"It truly was our pleasure," Greg said, shaking Charles's hand. "We've got a New Year's Eve party, too, if you're still in town."

"Greg makes the most incredible flourless chocolate cake," Sharon said with barely restrained excitement. "At the stroke of midnight, we cut the cake and celebrate the New Year."

"It's epic," Nathan threw in.

"Oh, well…" Though Sophia had been unsuccessful in determining a way for him to go back to his time, Charles was certain that there had to be some means of undoing the time travel. He had to apply himself to the task, and push away any possibility of failure.

Since he couldn't be certain where—or when—he'd be on New Year's Eve, making plans with the Turners seemed rather thoughtless and rude.

"Charles might be out of town," Megan said quickly.

"That's too bad." Greg looked disappointed, but recovered enough to say, "Give me your e-mail and I'll send you my cookie recipe, like you asked."

"E-mail?" What a peculiar word.

The Turners looked mystified at his puzzlement.

"He doesn't have a smartphone," Megan said, "And his computer is in the shop. Maybe just write it down later and I'll give it to him."

Charles tried to look as though he understood what she was saying, but even a few nights of watching television hadn't fully explained to him the strangeness of this century.

"Sure," Greg said.

After Charles shook hands with Nathan and Greg,

he took Sharon's hand, but instead of shaking it, he bent down and pressed a kiss to her knuckles.

"Oh, my," Sharon said, her other hand fluttering over her chest.

"It has been my extreme pleasure. Thank you for your cordiality and taking me into your home."

"Any time, Charles," Sharon said with sincerity.

He did the same with Elena, kissing her hand.

"Hey, man, don't make me look bad," Nathan said and laughed.

"Don't worry, *mi amor*." Elena slipped her hand from Charles's and snuggled close to her husband. "There's room in my heart for just one gallant knight, and that's you."

Charles struggled to swallow around the lump in his throat as he took in the Turner family. They had made him so welcome, treating him as though he was one of them. He hadn't felt this sense of belonging in…

He couldn't remember.

Certainly before the death of his parents.

Clearing his throat, he gestured for Megan to lead them toward the front door. But before they made it outside, both of their feet on the threshold, Nathan called out.

"Not so fast, you two."

Charles and Megan froze.

Nathan pointed to the top of the doorway. A sprig of mistletoe hung there, tied with a cheery red ribbon.

Charles's stomach dropped. *Oh, dear.*

"Come on! Charles is my *friend*." Megan's face was nearly as red as the ribbon around the berries.

A thread of indignation unwound in Charles's chest. She seemed awfully unwilling to kiss him. Perhaps he should be offended.

He would never kiss her without her permission, yet the idea of putting his lips to hers was...quite agreeable. More than agreeable.

"A gentleman never imposes his will on anyone," he said, searching for a polite way to end the discussion. Besides, if he and Megan kissed, he might find it exceedingly pleasant. And addicting.

"Well, it *is* tradition," Megan said. She looked at Charles. "Would you mind, if we...?"

"I wouldn't mind a bit," he said, too quickly to be nonchalant.

He and Megan faced each other. He looked down at her, and her eyes were wide, her lips parted. His heart beat furiously as though he'd been running at top speed, desperate to get somewhere, and now he'd arrived at his destination.

Megan lifted herself up on her toes, bracing her hands on his chest. The contact of her palms against him, even through his coat, sweater, and shirt, was a jolt of pure electricity.

Her eyes drifted shut, and he closed his eyes as well.

And then...

Her lips brushed against his.

It was a soft, sweet kiss. And yet he had the sensation

173

of being shot into the ether, floating high above the world. He'd never known such dizzying happiness. It felt far too good. Her lips held the slightest flavor of cocoa and ginger, making him long for more.

Too soon, she pulled back—though not all the way, with her hands still splayed on his chest.

"Oh, wow," she said on a breath.

"My sentiments exactly."

A light flashed and there was a clicking sound. Charles and Megan turned to see Nathan pointing his phone in their direction.

"*That* is going on Instagram," he said with a wide smile.

It was a measure of Charles's befuddlement that he didn't wonder what an *Instagram* was. He'd also forgotten that he and Megan had an audience—her family.

"Very funny, Nate," Megan said.

She put more distance between herself and Charles. Her eyes were very bright, almost feverish, but Charles suspected that he had the same fever.

"Our hybrid carriage awaits," she said.

"Good night," he said over his shoulder.

"Merry Christmas!" the Turners cried in unison, just before Megan shut the door decisively.

She hurried toward her automobile and fumbled for her keys.

"Sorry about that," she muttered.

I'm not.

CHAPTER TWELVE

Somehow, Megan managed to summon enough mental balance to drive Charles back to the mansion. It wasn't easy, though. A taut silence reigned in the car, and even the Christmas music playing on the radio couldn't quite distract her from the fact that she and Charles had kissed.

It would have been much smarter to have just ignored tradition and walked out from under the mistletoe without kissing him. That way, she couldn't torment herself with thoughts of how wonderful the kiss had been, how blissfully perfect, making her wish for things that would never—could never—happen.

She'd kissed him right in front of her family. Could things be more awkward?

He'd kissed her because they had been under the mistletoe. She shouldn't confuse honoring a tradition with anything else, and certainly not affection.

But he doesn't do *tradition, remember?*

She fought a groan as she turned onto the cul-desac in front of the mansion. Thinking herself in circles was getting her nowhere. Better to just chalk the kiss up to a friendly Christmas peck, and leave it at that.

She brought the car to a stop, and cleared her throat.

"Feels a little weird," she said, breaking the quiet, "knowing you're all alone in that big house."

"It won't be forever." He glanced out the window to look at the mansion's façade, bedecked with period-appropriate decorations. "I'll go back to my time, and then I'll have a house full of staff. And Eliza, of course."

"Of course. Eliza."

It sounded a lot like she and Charles were trying to remind themselves of Eliza's existence and how significant she was to him. Or maybe he was letting Megan know that, for all intents and purposes, he was engaged.

She wouldn't be the person who came between someone and their intended. That was out of the question.

"Sophia said she couldn't find anything in my journal to help return me to my time," he said after another pause.

"I'm sorry." Hopefully, Megan sounded more sincere than she felt.

"I know we'll figure out another way. This is not where I'm meant to be. I simply cannot tolerate the idea that Moran took possession of the house I had built, or inhabiting my life. It's unendurable."

She nodded, even though the movement made her whole body hurt.

"Did you have a good time tonight?" she asked. "The Christmas party, I mean, and going to the theater. I didn't mean the kiss. No. That's not what I meant at all. The party and the theater. That's what I'm asking about."

Please, stop talking, she begged herself.

If he noticed her babbling, he was too much of a gentleman to mention it.

"Actually," he said with surprise in his voice, "I did. The plays were thoroughly entertaining, but spending time with your family was the best part, I believe."

"That's what happens when you let people in. Good things happen."

"I'm beginning to see the logic in that." He fell silent, and she could only guess at what he was thinking. "So, about that letter of recommendation—"

"Oh, no." Not at all what she thought he was going to say. She leaned forward and tapped her forehead against the steering wheel. "Not this again."

"Yes, this again." He faced her. "I'm going to remind you over and over. If this is something you want, you ought to go after it. You gave the exact same advice to Amber earlier tonight, remember?"

With her head still on the steering wheel, she turned to look at him.

"Amber's super talented."

"As are you."

"You've never seen me teach," she fired back.

"But I've seen you with the tour groups. That's very similar to teaching."

Megan sat up. "I just don't have the nerve to get that letter. Maybe Professor Coyle hasn't gotten back to me because she doesn't want to write it. Maybe she thinks I'm not qualified, and is too polite to say so."

"Or," he said, raising a finger, "maybe she's simply overworked, as many academics are, and needs reminding. Just as you need reminding that you have Rosie's grit and determination. She had backbone—the same way you do."

"Heavens, let me be the person you believe I am."

His gaze was level as it held hers.

"You can't succeed in business if you aren't a good judge of character."

"And you're an excellent judge of character?"

"Precisely."

"I'll give it some thought," she said, just to end the conversation. With the topic of the letter of recommendation exhausted, thoughts of the Christmas party—and the kiss—came flooding back in.

She made herself hold the steering wheel rather than reach for his hand to weave their fingers together.

"I guess I'll see you tomorrow," she said with forced cheeriness.

He let out a breath. "Good night."

It was better to just go before she said or did anything she would regret.

"Good night. And thanks for coming to the party

and being such a good sport about it. You know, with the hats."

"It truly was my pleasure." He hesitated for a moment, and then opened the car door before climbing out and closing the door behind him.

She gave him a wave before quickly pulling away. If she didn't drive off, she might attempt something truly ridiculous—like asking him to stay in 2018.

Usually, Megan's morning run cleared her mind. There was something so calming about being out just before the sunrise, with only herself and a few hardy (or foolish) souls out, and the day full of unrealized potential.

She especially loved morning runs during the winter, when the fallen snow made everything hushed and crisp. After indulging in so many of her dad's cookies last night, she could use the cardio, too.

But as she finished her run with her usual stop at Tina's Diner, Megan's mind was anything but clear.

Plucking the earbuds from her ears—playing her favorite '90s rock—she slid into a seat at the counter. Moments later, Tina appeared in a cute holiday apron with a carafe of coffee in her hand.

"Fill you up?" Tina asked.

"Yes, please," Megan said distractedly.

Tina poured Megan a cup. "What else can I get you? Your usual sticky rice? Banana pancakes?"

"Huh?"

Tina waved a hand in front of Megan's face. "Hellooo! Maybe I should wait for you to ingest some caffeine before asking hard-hitting questions."

Megan shook her head. "Sorry. I'm a little distracted."

"It happens, especially this time of year." Tina waved at a departing postal worker before turning her attention back to Megan. "Got the holiday blues?"

"More like an existential crisis."

Tina whistled. "Those are never convenient."

"They sure aren't." Megan dumped some creamer into her coffee and gave it a stir. "Did you always know that you wanted to own a restaurant?"

"There was a period between the fourth and fifth grade when I seriously considered working at a wildlife park with live dinosaurs, and a brief high school flirtation with joining a heavy metal band. But mostly, I knew I loved feeding people."

"Was it hard work, starting up the diner?"

Tina gave a low, rueful chuckle. "If anybody ever tells you how easy and relaxed it is to get a restaurant off the ground, check their pupils to make sure they don't have a concussion."

Megan grimaced. "Tough, huh?"

"The toughest. So many obstacles to overcome, so many hoops to jump through. Loans and permits and inspections." She shook her head.

"But you knew it was worth it," Megan said.

"Sure. Sticking my neck out was risky, but I saw that it had to be done, or else my dream of Tina's

Diner would never come true." Tina's brow furrowed in concern. "Everything okay, working with Phil at the Whitley-Moran place? My kid brother can be kind of a pain in the neck sometimes."

"Phillip's great," Megan said without hesitation. "And I love working at the mansion. But…"

"It's not what you want to be doing for the rest of your life."

"Exactly." Megan propped her chin in her hand. "There's something standing in the way of getting what I want, but I'm not sure I can make myself take that step to overcome it. I just…don't have the mettle."

It was so hard to admit that, to give voice to the doubts that had been pestering her. When she'd talked with Amber, it had seemed so much easier. Amber wanted to audition for Broadway, so she should go for it. It seemed so different for Megan, as though there was no way around or over the obstacles in her path.

However, for all Megan's indecisiveness, Tina looked at her with empathy, not judgment.

If only Megan could spare herself that same judgment.

"I get it," Tina said. "And I also have a memory of you selling lemonade outside your folks' house. Never mind that it was December and twenty degrees out. You were going to sell that lemonade."

They both chuckled.

"My dad wasn't crazy about the idea," Megan murmured. "Still, he helped me build the stand and a sign. And Nate made all his friends buy some lemonade—even though it had frozen in the cups." She sighed. "I used to not know the meaning of 'no.' I used to not stand in my own way."

"So what changed?"

Megan frowned. "I don't want to keep you from your other customers."

"Look around," Tina said, and laughed. "It's just us, Billy the cook, and a long-haul trucker, and he's fallen asleep."

Megan turned in her seat to see a man sitting in a booth, his head nodding as his oatmeal got cold.

There was no way to avoid thinking or talking about her reasons for holding back.

"I think I started second-guessing myself," Megan said after mulling it over. "There were people in my PhD program who were so outspoken, so driven. If I wanted to say anything in a seminar, I'd have to shout over them. It was just easier to keep my head down and be quiet. And then there was Brandon."

Tina growled. "That loser. Coming in here, talking on speakerphone and telling *me* how to make Vietnamese coffee. Plus," she added hotly, "he was dumb enough to break up with the best person in his life."

"Aw." Megan reached out and squeezed Tina's hand. Warmth moved through her. "Thanks. For some reason, I believed him when he said I was too boring and too nice to get anywhere."

"The guy wore his sunglasses inside, and I *know* he didn't have an eye condition. So, it's safe to assume that his opinion is pretty much worthless."

182

Megan couldn't help but laugh. "You've got a point."

"You bet I do!"

"I wish I wasn't so self-critical."

Tina looked at her with disbelief. "You're getting down on yourself for getting down on yourself. Not exactly the most rational train of thought."

"I guess not!" Megan chuckled. It did seem kind of silly to hear Tina describe it that way.

"Now, let's get some food into you so I can at least pretend like I'm working."

Tina's Diner specialized in both amazing traditional diner fare as well as incredible Vietnamese food, so Megan was more than happy to place her order for a *banh mi* sandwich with a fried egg.

As she ate her breakfast, she wondered if all the negative thoughts in her head weren't really her own thoughts. Maybe they were actually other people's opinions. Besides, thoughts weren't facts. They were just thoughts.

But then there was Charles, and his unshakable notion that she and Rosie were both spunky spitfires. Perhaps that wasn't such a crazy idea.

After finishing up and giving Tina a farewell hug, Megan walked home. In the early morning hours, the town was peaceful and hushed, as if waiting for something to happen.

I know the feeling.

She passed Mr. Burgess walking his two dogs. The two pets were of unknown breeds, since they had been adopted from the animal shelter, but it was clear in the way they looked at Mr. Burgess that they felt nothing but love and gratitude for him.

"Hey, guys," she said, bending down to give the dogs head scratches. "You taking your human for a walk?"

"They love the snow," Mr. Burgess said, his voice slightly muffled by his thick scarf.

"You guys should build a snow doggie," Megan said. "Too bad they don't have any thumbs."

"They'll get over it, especially when I feed them their favorite organic, grain-free snacks." He pulled his scarf down a little so she could hear him better. "Looking forward to the party at the mansion!"

"I'm so glad you'll be there." Many of Cutter Springs's residents turned up at the house's holiday gathering, and it always made Megan smile to see how close-knit the community was.

"I never miss it," Mr. Burgess said, his grin poking out from the top of his scarf.

The dogs pulled at their leashes, eager to be on their way.

"Looks like they're ready to hit the road," Megan said. She gave Mr. Burgess a wave. "See you at the party!"

Once she'd parted company with Mr. Burgess and his dogs, she walked home, her limbs moving just as quickly as her thoughts. She mulled over what Tina had said, just as she thought about Charles's encouragement. Was it hypocritical of her to urge Amber to audition but hold back, herself?

She reached her apartment and showered quickly, her mind churning.

If she didn't get that letter, she couldn't apply for the position. That meant she'd stay at the mansion for who knew how long, leading tours. While she loved her work at the house, it wasn't her dream. She longed to be in front of a lecture hall, introducing students to the expansive and incredible world of American history, and exploring both its triumphs and its darker moments. There was something almost magical about seeing minds opening and learning, and for *her* to make that happen…it was thrilling.

I have to go for it.

If she didn't, she'd spend her life wondering, *What if…?* Meeting Charles had taught her that time was precious and you couldn't spend it fretting or, in her case, sabotaging yourself. She didn't want to look back at her time on Earth and feel a sense of regret. Too much was out of your control, but some things you *could* shape.

This was one of those things that was in her hands.

After she dried her hair and got dressed, she chose her clothes with care. Today was important. She wanted to look professional and competent.

She lingered in front of the mirror in the entryway of her apartment. A quick rehearsal might help a little.

Giving in to a strange impulse, she put on the

cap she wore when playing Rosie, and drew on the woman's self-assurance as she looked at her reflection.

"Professor Coyle," she said to herself, "I hate to bother you…"

Not strong enough.

"Would it be too much trouble, Professor, if you wrote me that letter of recommendation like you promised?"

That's not it! Channel your inner Rosie!

"Professor Coyle," she said, lifting up her chin, "I would appreciate it if you wrote the letter of recommendation and had it in my inbox by the end of the week."

Better.

Firm and assertive without being pushy. Exactly what Rosie might say.

Megan pulled the cap off and looked at it. Confidence surged through her. This *wasn't* impossible. And while Tina and Charles had provided support, she'd make it happen for herself.

"Thanks, Rosie, for helping me out," she murmured aloud. "I think I've got it from here."

After taking a breath, she put the cap in her purse, grabbed her coat, and headed out the door.

Her next stop: the History Building at the university.

CHAPTER THIRTEEN

It felt strange for Charles to limit his non-work activities to a few rooms in what was a vast property. Only a few days ago, he'd had the run of his house, and no room was off-limits to him, no matter the hour. If he wanted to play ninepins in the ballroom wearing only his pajamas, he could have done so. The house was *his*. He'd built it, and paid for every brick and pane of glass.

Yet in this modern era, he kept to a handful of rooms. True, Phillip was the museum manager, and he understood that Charles had a perfect right to roam wherever he wanted. But this was also the staff's place of work, and they toiled considerably to keep everything pristine and in its specific place.

His altered perception also served as a reminder that the person he had been in 1902 and the person he was over a hundred years in the future were not the same. He'd grown and changed—thanks to Megan. He would make many changes when he returned to his time, not just to the house, but to himself, and his relationships.

While he was here, however, there was something important that required his attention.

It was early in the morning as he sat with his tools in the museum's staff room. Hopefully, it was early enough that Megan wouldn't come in and interrupt his work. His efforts were for her, after all.

Though his hands were busy as he tinkered with a number of small mechanical devices, his mind was even more active. It was nearly impossible to think of anything else but last night's kiss under the mistletoe.

Telling himself that it was merely custom didn't absolve him of the fact that he had enjoyed the kiss far too much. He'd wanted it to last much longer. She'd been gentle and sweet, and his heart had pounded like an engine when her lips had touched his.

Thoughts of Eliza popped into his mind and the pleasure he'd felt in kissing Megan evaporated like the steam from the engine.

He was a cad. Eliza deserved far better than a wayward fiancé. And Megan deserved better than a man who toyed with her affections while promised to another.

It can't happen a second time. He wouldn't permit it, no matter how much he wanted to kiss Megan again.

The screwdriver in his hand jumped, and he nearly stabbed his hand with its tip. He cursed softly to himself. More than anything, right now he needed *focus*. Especially if he wanted to return to his own time.

That was what he wanted, of course. To go back and make everything right. It was his responsibility to return to his own era. Eliza was there, and they'd planned a life together.

And Harold Moran could not be permitted to supplant Charles.

He still hadn't figured out how to accomplish his return, however. Truth was, he'd been so busy enjoying his time here that he hadn't truly applied himself to the problem.

"Hey, Charles," Dan said cheerily as he strolled into the staff room. He went straight to the pot of coffee and poured some for himself. "Lots of fun last night at the Turners'. Their holiday hat tradition is always the best. Ready to learn about the wonders of the internet?"

Charles barely managed a distracted grunt as he continued to labor over the mechanical pieces.

"Where'd you get those tools?" Dan asked, sitting down on the other side of the table.

"I had them custom-made for me by a clockmaker in Zurich."

"Did they travel with you from 1902?"

Charles angled a wry look up at Dan. "In a manner. I always kept them in a compartment in my desk which hasn't been touched in over a hundred years. I took a chance that they might still be in there, and they were." He gave Dan a rueful smile. "We don't need to mention this to Phillip. He takes his job as my home's guardian very seriously."

Dan mimed locking his mouth shut. But then he peered closer at the array of metal pieces spread out over the table. Charles had laid them out atop a towel so he wouldn't scratch the table's surface.

"Seems like you're building a time-travel device," Dan said. "Though I have to say, I don't know what a time-travel device looks like. Maybe it looks like a toaster oven, but instead of dialing in how dark you want your toast, you pick how far in time you want to go. Say," Dan exclaimed, sitting up straight, "that's not a bad idea."

"Could get rather messy," Charles said. "You simply want your breakfast and instead, wind up having your tea with Catherine the Great."

"Good point. So, what are you building?"

Charles busied himself with making minute adjustments to the tension on a coil. He muttered something under his breath.

"Sorry, I didn't catch that." Dan leaned closer.

"It's a surprise. For Megan."

With a look of speculation, Dan leaned back in his chair and sipped at his coffee. "Interesting."

"I'm not going to explore what *interesting* means," Charles grumbled.

"All I'm saying is that you and Megan seem very close."

"We're friends," Charles said in a clipped voice.

One of Dan's eyebrows lifted up. "Do *friends* make surprise inventions for *friends*?"

Charles set his tools down and got to his feet. He

needed to move, and being hunched over these bits of metal certainly didn't help quell the restlessness that pushed him from the inside out.

He strode to the window of the staff room and looked out at the snowy fields surrounding the mansion. Truly, there wasn't a bad view anywhere in the house, which had been part of his intent when sketching out its design for his team of architects. He had wanted to impress everyone—even the servants, since this room had been designated for their use. But he saw now that he'd been trying to create a beautiful home, a place where one could find nourishment for the soul. He'd wanted to share with Eliza what he had been able to accomplish. They would have raised their family here, amidst the loveliness of the rolling hills and pine forests.

But in the wake of his disappearance, Eliza had married Harold Moran. She and Moran had brought up their children in the home Charles had built.

Charles couldn't let Moran win. The idea made Charles's throat close up and his pulse hammer with anger. That knave wasn't entitled to anything that Charles had built or created.

The joys of this house did not belong to Moran. They belonged to Charles.

And…Megan worked here. Megan loved this place, which made him happy. Anything that gave her joy made him happy.

The realization hit him like a shock of electricity. *Oh, no.*

191

He glanced over his shoulder, making certain that he and Dan were alone.

"I may have…" He cleared his throat. "…feelings for Megan."

Dan was beside him in an instant, slapping his shoulder. "Buddy, that's great! You two seem really perfect for each other."

"It is *not* great." Charles felt his brow lower. "My feelings cannot progress because I will be returning to my own time. It wouldn't be fair to tell her how I feel, and then leave."

The grin Dan sported fell. "Oh, yeah. That makes sense."

"Precisely. I am not a scoundrel, and would never hurt her that way."

"I know you aren't," Dan said quietly. "How *are* you getting back to your time, anyway?"

"That, I cannot answer. Not yet. But I vow that I'll find some means of doing so." He'd been turning it over and over, wearing the hard rock of the conundrum into a smooth pebble, and yet he'd found no solution.

"Sophia's still pretty mad at herself for not being able to find a way to get you home."

"I told her not to be cross with herself," Charles said. "Even Edison and Tesla would have been stymied by such an enigma."

"True, but she holds herself to a pretty high standard."

Charles smirked. "I wonder where she gets that characteristic from?"

Dan rolled his eyes, but then said in a tentative voice, "Maybe you should stay. In this time. You've got a good job, and friends, and Megan."

"No." Charles knotted his hands into fists as resentment tightened his body. Whenever he thought of Moran seated at the dining table in *his* home, or taking a walk around the grounds, anger choked him. Forcefully, he said, "I must get back to 1902 and prevent Harold Moran from taking over my life."

"*That's* the reason why you want to return to your time? To defeat your rival?" Dan looked dubious.

"Dislike is a powerful motivator."

"So is love," Dan said.

Charles stared at Dan, absorbing his friend's words. He could not fully process their meaning, his heart and mind instinctively shying away from things that were too big, too significant.

Was it possible? Was what he felt for Megan more than just friendship? Whenever he thought of her, peace settled over him like the caress of a summer breeze. Being with her gave him a buoyant sensation—happiness. He was happy when he was with her, delighting in every moment and not planning on being somewhere else, or thinking about the next innovation or business strategy. He simply wanted to be in that moment with her.

Charles nearly groaned aloud.

He couldn't allow himself to be derailed from his goal by something as complicated—as rare and fragile—as love.

If only he could shut it into a box, lock it away, and bury the key. But emotions didn't function that way. They were complex and disorderly and threw everything into confusion.

His heart leapt when, a moment later, Megan strolled into the staff room.

"Good morning!" she sang as she entered. There was a decided spring in her step, a new confidence, and a small smile played about her lips. She looked decidedly lovely.

And there it was, the happiness he felt whenever she was near.

Oh, drat.

In fact, Charles was so taken by the pleasure that radiated from her that he almost forgot to hide the evidence of his surprise. Almost.

He lunged for the table where the mechanical devices were arrayed, and gathered up the corners of the towel to create a bundle that he carefully cradled.

"What's that?" she asked, eyeing the bundle.

"Dan asked me to repair an alarm clock," Charles said at once.

"He could always use his phone if he needs an alarm."

"They can do that, too?"

Dan leapt in. "It's an antique."

"Oh, can I see your progress?" Megan took a step forward. "I've read about the development of the alarm clock. Did you know that the Seth Thomas Clock Company patented the bedside mechanical windup alarm clock in 1876? Before that, home clocks were expensive so most people relied on church bells or factory whistles to indicate what time it was." Her cheeks turned a charming shade of pink. "I'm history-babbling again."

"You have considerable knowledge," Charles said, adoring her enthusiasm. "That's something to be proud of."

She thought about it for a moment, then lifted her chin. "You're right. I *should* feel proud of myself." She looked at the bundle once more. "So, can I see?"

Charles thrust the towel and its contents behind his back.

"I prefer not to show my work until it's completed." He had, in truth, often consulted with fellow innovators and engineers in the midst of a project—yet she didn't need to know that.

"Got it."

She and Charles stared at each other for a long moment. He was flooded with remembrance of how soft her lips had been, the wonder of their kiss, and how much he wanted to do it again.

I am in deep trouble.

It seemed she was entertaining the same thoughts, because the flush in her cheeks darkened.

"Uh," Dan said, and cleared his throat, reminding Charles that he and Megan were not alone. "Great party last night."

Megan blinked, breaking the spell between her and Charles.

"Thanks for coming," she said. "My folks love it when we cram in as many people as possible into our little house. Good thing occupancy limits don't apply to private residences. I think."

"I found myself missing my courtier's hat this morning," Charles said. "The feather, in particular."

She smiled at him, and his heart pounded. *Going back to 1902, remember? Returning to my time, and to Eliza.*

A moment later, Amber entered the staff room. She clutched the book of monologues to her chest as she approached Megan.

Charles took advantage of the distraction to set his bundle aside.

"Hey," Amber said, "so, I've been thinking a lot about what you said. About how I need to share my talent with people."

"Not just *people*," Megan said. "The *world*."

"Well, first I have to share it with the casting director so…" Amber scrunched up her nose. "Would it be too much trouble if you helped me video my audition?"

Megan's eyes went wide. "You're going for it?"

"I am." Amber looked a little stunned, yet she smiled bravely.

"That's great!" Megan quickly stepped forward and embraced Amber.

"Is there any way I can be of assistance?" Charles asked. "Anything to help the theatrical world to discover your ability."

Amber smiled at Charles. "Thanks. I suppose I'll

need to rehearse—maybe you and Megan could watch and give me some tips?"

"My own experience with the theater is, admittedly, rather limited, but I shall be happy to support your endeavor."

"How about tonight, after work?" Megan suggested. "I'll order pizza, we'll help you rehearse, and then we'll shoot and edit your video."

"That sounds great." Amber flashed them an anxious look. "I'm so nervous. I've never auditioned for anything this big before."

"You're going to do splendidly," Charles said with authority.

"Knock 'em dead," Dan added.

A chirping noise sounded from Megan's pocket.

She pulled out her phone, poked her finger at the screen, and then let out a yelp that nearly made Charles jump.

"Oh my goodness!" she cried. "That was…that was fast!"

"What was fast?" Dan asked.

Charles moved to her side, panic spiking along his spine. "Are you all right? Is something wrong?"

"I'm fine, I'm fine." She was breathing heavily, though, and looked at him with wide eyes. "It's Professor Coyle. She just sent me her letter of recommendation."

"That's wonderful," Charles exclaimed. His panic quickly shifted to excitement and joy, especially seeing the happiness in her face.

She'd done it. He thought his chest would burst with pleasure. Never had he felt prouder, not even when he had been profiled by *The Wall Street Journal.*

Seeing someone else he cared about succeed was much more gratifying than achieving something just for himself.

"Oh my goodness!" Amber exclaimed. She pressed her fingertips to her mouth.

Dan held his arms open. "I think this calls for a celebratory hug."

Immediately, Megan went to Dan and wrapped her arms around him.

"Thank you," she said, her voice still somewhat dazed.

When she and Dan stepped apart, Amber swooped in and also hugged her.

After Amber released her, Megan looked at Charles uncertainly.

"Two friends can embrace, surely," he said. "Especially when congratulations are in order."

He opened his arms. When Megan stepped into them, he tried to tell himself that he was merely being friendly. He'd do the same for anyone.

Though that wasn't true. He wasn't the kind of man to spontaneously—or intentionally—hug people. Yet it felt right and natural with Megan. He was at peace with her, sensing the beating of her heart against his, as if they had achieved perfect synchronicity. He inhaled her lovely light, floral scent.

Somewhere, he'd heard that scent triggered memory

more than any other sense. If that was so, he wanted to breathe her fragrance in deeply.

She fit well in his arms, too. As if she was meant to be there.

Her hands splayed on his back as she clasped him, and he thought she nuzzled close to his neck. His nerves tightened to attention.

She gave him an extra squeeze. That was *not* in his imagination.

Could it be…had she feelings for him, too?

He dared not hope.

Besides, he sternly reminded himself, whatever affections they had for each other could not develop. He had to return to his time, had to make everything right and reclaim his life, to stop Moran from muscling in on what should have belonged to Charles. Then he and Megan would be separated by over a century.

"Ahem," Dan said.

Only then did Charles realize he was still embracing Megan. At once, he dropped his arms and put distance between them.

Her pupils had gone wide, and she blinked as if collecting herself.

"Felicitations," he said sincerely. "How wonderful that Professor Coyle finally took action."

"She did have a little prompting," Megan said. "I thought about what you've been saying to me, and how I needed to channel my inner Rosie. But then I realized, I didn't have to pretend to be anyone else."

She smiled widely. "I'm good enough on my own to get what I want."

"Amazing!" Amber exclaimed.

"That is sincerely wonderful," Charles said. Thank goodness that Megan was able to recognize her own value.

Megan didn't duck her head or look abashed. Instead, she accepted the praise with a raised chin and straight shoulders.

"We should celebrate," Dan said. "Tonight, after you guys do Amber's audition video. We'll go to Tina's for her peppermint cheesecake."

Megan hopped up and down. "Yes! Bring Lydia and Sophia. We can celebrate together." She turned an expectant gaze to Charles.

His heart soared, and then hurtled back toward the earth.

"I would like to," he said softly. "More than anything. But…" He exhaled. "I ought to delve further into how I can return to 1902."

He already struggled against the emotional ties that bound him to this time. Returning to 1902 promised to be painful enough, but the more time he spent with Amber, Dan, Sophia, and the Turners and…Megan…the greater the thought of voyaging through the decades to his own era felt like he was being torn in two.

He couldn't have it both ways. He couldn't allow himself to grow invested in this era, in caring about her, and then blithely travel back to the past. It would hurt them both.

"Oh." Megan's tone was flat and sad, and he hated that he was responsible for that sadness. "That makes sense. I just thought, since you helped me get the letter—"

"That was all your doing," he said. "I merely offered a minimum of encouragement. You did the most difficult part on your own."

"I did," she said after a moment. "I did do it on my own."

She smiled, and though it was warm and sincere, her eyes remained despondent.

CHAPTER FOURTEEN

Working that day helped ground Megan as she cycled between elation and unhappiness. She guided tours through the house, pointing out the beautiful carved ceilings as her spirit soared high—*I got the letter!*—and then she drew visitors' attention to the intricately inlaid floors, where her heart would lay morosely—*he still wants to leave.*

As guests posed in front of the giant, decorated fir tree in the ballroom, taking selfies as the countless mirrors reflected their smiling faces, she stood back and watched, feeling the glum little smile on her lips.

"Rosie," one of the visitors said, holding out their phone, "could you take a picture of us all together?"

"I'll just pretend this implement is one of Mr. Eastman's photographic devices." She took the phone and stepped back so that she could get the entire group in the frame. "Say 'Happy Holidays!'"

"Happy Holidays," everyone called out.

She pressed the button and the image on the

screen froze. After checking the photo to make sure everyone's eyes were open, she gave the phone back. The crowd broke up as they investigated all the lovely details of the ballroom, from the carved cornices to the imported French mirrors.

"This place is awesome," a little boy said as his parents admired the decorated tree in the middle of the room.

"We think so, too." But the spectacle of the mansion decorated for Christmas wasn't awesome enough to keep Charles here. And, apparently, neither was she.

You're not being fair.

She hadn't said anything to him about her growing feelings for him, and it was a tremendous thing to ask him to stay for her sake—especially with his whole life waiting for him back in 1902.

"If everyone will come with me," she said to the visitors, "I can show you the billiards room that has three full-sized mahogany billiards tables, custom-made for Mr. Whitley in St. Louis."

She made her way down the corridor, talking over her shoulder as she did so.

"Mr. Whitley had the billiards balls made of celluloid—a form of plastic—because he was concerned about the use of ivory. Did you know, however, that these celluloid balls had a habit of exploding?"

"No way," the little boy exclaimed.

She nodded. "It's true. Celluloid is made with nitrocellulose, as well as flash paper and gun cotton.

Which means that sometimes, when two balls hit each other just right…BANG!" She clapped her hands together, and the guests all jumped.

After collecting themselves, everyone chuckled.

"Pretty cool," the boy said. "Can we get some?" he asked his mother.

"Absolutely not," came the definitive answer.

As Megan continued on with the tour, she let herself coast on the warm sense of accomplishment she always got when someone, especially a child, enjoyed the history she told them. It might spark a lasting interest in history. Or maybe, in the boy's case, he'd become fascinated by the sciences and discover things that would revolutionize the world.

After the billiards room, Megan showed the visitors more of the house, and they had their encounters with the butler and Eliza.

Then it was time to meet Mr. Whitley himself. The tour had been reordered so that they now finished with the study. Meeting Charles was the high note of the visit.

As they entered the study, she made herself smile at Charles. Still, she couldn't repress the sting of his decision not to join tonight's celebration.

"What are you doing?" he demanded as she and the visitors came into the room. "Why are you escorting strangers into my private study?"

She and Charles quickly fell into their patter. It felt so comfortable, so effortless. They didn't have to work hard to harmonize with each other. And when he answered the guests' questions, he did so graciously, as if he really did enjoy talking with them.

Why can't *he stay? He likes it here, and maybe…he likes me.*

It was his choice, and she had to respect that. She managed to collect herself enough to guide the visitors out when they'd asked their last question.

"I want to tell you something," he said, just after the final guest left the room. "Something important."

"Later, Charles." She didn't mean to snap at him, but it wasn't easy to recognize that the person she cared about didn't feel as deeply about her.

"Oh." He blinked, likely caught off guard by her tone. "Yes, later."

She couldn't even muster a weary smile before leaving the study. At least she could bury herself in her responsibilities as a tour guide rather than sitting and moping. Moping never helped anything.

When the last guests departed, Megan walked slowly back to the staff room. Maybe she wouldn't go out to celebrate after helping Amber with her audition tape. She could just go home, put on her snuggliest sweater and sweatpants, and finish her historical romance novel.

She shook her head at herself. No. She wouldn't let some unwanted feelings get in the way of a celebration.

Stepping into the staff room, she found Charles, Dan, Amber, and Phillip. They all looked at her excitedly.

"What's up?" she asked.

"Charles thinks he has an idea about how he traveled through time," Dan said.

"Is that what you were trying to tell me earlier?" she asked.

He nodded.

"I'm sorry for being so rude." Now she felt like a jerk.

"No need to trouble yourself. It was an inopportune moment."

"Tell me about this way to go back in time."

His hands moving animatedly as he spoke. "The key component is the clock I brought back from Paris."

"Really?"

He hurried out of the staff room and toward his study. Everyone followed.

They gathered in the room, standing in a semicircle in front of the broken clock.

"I was tinkering with this," Charles said, pointing to the timepiece. "Attempting to fix it. I had gotten the clock to work for a moment when a piece sprang free, and that's when the time travel happened."

"Is the piece there now?" Phillip asked.

Charles bent close and examined the clock. "It's gone."

"Maybe it's around somewhere," Megan said. "Eliza preserved this wing of the house almost immediately after you disappeared. It could still be here."

"Everyone," Charles said, holding out his hands, "split up. We'll comb this room. Perhaps fate will be kind to us and that piece will turn up. Look for a very small piece that looks like a coil."

The group dispersed through the study. They looked high and low, opening cabinets, lifting rugs, pulling books out of the shelves, and searching every inch.

Megan got onto her hands and knees, poking into the corners and examining the baseboards. As she did, part of her hoped for success, and another part—the part she wasn't proud of—prayed for failure. If the piece stayed missing, maybe Charles would have to stay.

But no. If he remained in the present, she wanted it to be because he chose to, not because he had to.

She bent lower to look beneath a very heavy chest pushed against the wall.

Her heart jumped into her throat as she glimpsed the shine of something metallic. Was that it?

She managed to get her fingers beneath the chest, and was barely able to grab the piece with the very tips of her fingers. They closed around something made of metal.

She pulled it out and cradled it in her palm. It was a tiny thing, just a little coil, hardly looking like something with power over time.

But she knew deep down that it was the key.

Before she could give in to the temptation to throw the piece away, she stood. "I found it."

Everyone gathered around her, their voices mingling in exclamations of surprise and excitement.

Megan held the piece out to Charles, who stepped

forward with a look of wonderment and plucked the piece from her hand.

"It's a spiral torsion spring," he murmured. "The clock won't work without it."

"But you've got it now," Dan said.

"Which means you can fix the clock and go back to your time," Amber added.

A silence fell, and with it, Megan's heart sank. Her time with Charles was almost at an end. He'd return to where he belonged, to the life he was meant to have. And she'd go on with her own life, moving into the future without him beside her, encouraging her, making her laugh and feel like someone important.

She made herself smile. "Let's get you home!"

He looked strangely solemn as he approached the clock and bent over it, preparing to place the spring into its rightful place.

The room went still as everyone held their breaths.

"Wait," Megan heard herself say. When everybody looked at her with puzzled expressions, she said, "Before you go, I think we should all say goodbye."

"Yes. Of course." Charles turned to Phillip, his hand extended. "Thank you for your generosity and giving me some truly unforgettable employment."

"It's not every day that I can have a reenactor play himself," the museum manager said with a grin as he and Charles shook hands.

Then Charles turned to Amber. "You made an excellent Eliza."

"And you were a pretty good Charles," Amber said, then smiled.

"I have a good feeling about your audition."

Amber laughed. "You haven't seen it yet!"

"But I've seen you onstage. You'll bowl them over, and if they have a lick of sense, they'll cast you."

"Thanks, Charles." She hugged him.

Dan stepped forward. "I'm going to miss you, man. You're definitely a class act."

"The sentiment is mutual."

"I hope you can forgive me for being such a pain in the neck at the beginning."

Charles waved this off. "Your hostility was perfectly understandable."

"Glad there are no hard feelings."

"None. And please, tell Sophia that she should never give up her dreams. She's going to change the world one day."

"Oh, I know it." Dan shook Charles's hand. "Safe journey, Charles."

Then Charles turned to her.

They both stood in a silence fraught with unspoken emotion. She blinked back tears. This was it. The time when their paths, having briefly met, diverged once more. Letting him go was one of the hardest things she could imagine. She knew she'd survive it, but it was going to hurt worse than anything she'd ever faced before.

From his look of distress, she wasn't alone in that feeling.

"So…" she said. Words felt inadequate, yet she felt obliged to keep speaking them. "Goodbye."

"Farewell," he said quietly.

Neither of them moved.

"Oh, for Pete's sake!" Dan burst out. "Just hug already!"

She exhaled and stepped nearer to Charles. He closed the distance. And then they were hugging—just as they had hugged earlier in the day, only instead of celebrating, they were parting forever.

She closed her eyes tightly, trying to make herself commit to memory the feel of him.

"I won't forget you," he said softly.

"Same." She couldn't speak anything that would fully express the depth of her emotions. It seemed better, a little less painful, to keep things quick.

Before she gripped him harder and pleaded with him to stay, she moved back and pasted on an encouraging smile.

"Off you go!" she said with an attempt at cheeriness.

His lips pressed together as if he wanted to say more, but then he turned back to the clock. After letting out a breath, he wiggled the spring into place.

The room fell silent.

And then the clock began to tick.

Megan went motionless, waiting for the room to shake or a light to flash, waiting for Charles to disappear back to his own century.

Charles, too, held himself in readiness, standing

alertly as he balanced on the balls of his feet, his arms straight at his sides.

"Nothing's happening," Phillip whispered loudly to Dan.

"Give it a minute," Dan whispered back.

But the clock continued to tick, and Charles continued to stand in his study, very much present in the current era.

"I don't understand," Charles said, his brow furrowed in puzzlement. "The clock is working, and yet here I am."

"Maybe," Megan said, "something else needs to happen to trigger the time travel."

"Was something else happening the night you came forward in time?" Dan asked.

"Try retracing your steps," Phillip added, and Amber nodded.

Charles crossed his arms over his chest as he pondered the question.

Meanwhile, Megan tried as hard as she could not to feel too happy that he hadn't gone.

It's not fair to keep him here. Let him go back to his life.

"Let's see," he said thoughtfully. "I'd just returned from Paris. The staff had taken my trunks up to my room, and I entered this room so I might review my correspondence—including a letter from Eliza, inviting me to spend the holiday with her family. Rosie wanted me to go. But I told Rosie I was staying home, and dismissed her from the room."

He walked pensively around his desk, positioning himself behind it. "I was going to work on the clock. But before I did, I went to the window and looked out and…"

His brow cleared as a realization hit him.

"There was a full moon," he said animatedly. "A red moon. And an eclipse. There was a lunar eclipse that night!"

"So maybe," Megan said, "if the clock starts running and the eclipse happens at the same time, then you can travel back through time."

Dan, who had been busy on his phone, held it up. "The next red moon lunar eclipse is on Christmas Eve."

"That's tomorrow night," Phillip said.

Another astonished silence fell, interrupted only by the ticking of the clock. Suddenly the clock went quiet as Charles removed the spring and slipped it into his pocket.

"Then we wait until tomorrow," he said.

Megan stared at him, knowing that she couldn't keep the sadness from her eyes. She'd been ready to lose him, but knowing that their time together was nearing its end made everything that much more painful.

CHAPTER FIFTEEN

"Welcome, welcome!" Megan held open the front door of her apartment. She felt ridiculously nervous as Amber and Charles stepped across the threshold. Having Charles in her private space…that was new.

Amber came right in and, after pulling off her puffer jacket, started setting up. "I borrowed my aunt's video camera and tripod."

"Why does she have a video camera and a tripod?" Megan asked.

"To film all of her niece's performances, of course!"

Megan chuckled. "Makes sense."

"I brought my laptop, too," Amber continued, "so we can do everything this evening. The audition videos are due by midnight tonight—but I promise it won't take that long. There's the celebration at Tina's later, and I'll definitely be done by then."

"It's not a problem," Megan said. "Tina's is open late." She turned to Charles, who stood nervously in the small entryway, looking as though he was on the verge of bolting. "I can take your coat."

"Ah, thank you." But he didn't move. He flashed a self-conscious smile. "Forgive me. It's just that I'm not accustomed to being in a single woman's home."

"Right." She nodded. "Manners are a little more relaxed now, so there's no possibility of scandal. Besides, we have Amber as our chaperone."

Yet it was a little strange having him here, in her apartment. Thank goodness she'd tidied this evening before anyone came over, gathering up armfuls of papers and the occasional wrapper from a granola bar. When it was tidy, she felt pretty proud of her space, decorated with tonal shades of green and brown. Posters of nineteenth-century portraits and landscapes were framed and artfully arranged on the walls, and her collection of old patent medicine bottles had a home in an antique, glass-fronted cabinet.

Hopefully, Charles liked what he saw of her home.

That was silly. He was leaving tomorrow, and would never again set foot inside her apartment. But she wanted him to have good memories of her, including where she lived.

"That's right." Yet he still didn't remove his coat. "Apologies. It takes a bit of getting used to." He exhaled, and finally shucked his coat.

Megan took it from him and gathered Amber's outerwear, too. "I'll just put these away."

As she walked down the hallway to hang her guests' jackets up in the closet, she had to force herself not to bend close and sniff the collar of Charles's coat. Still, it looked and felt far too nice to hang his clothing next to hers. She closed the closet door with a snap so that she wouldn't be tempted to moon over the sight.

When she returned to the living room, Amber had affixed the camera to the tripod and was positioning it so that it faced a blank wall. Charles, however, seemed transfixed by Megan's many books. Bookshelves lined the whole living room, full nearly to bursting, and more books were piled up on the coffee table and nearly every other available surface.

"This is a substantial collection," he murmured.

"I've got books in literally every room of this apartment," she said. "On my bedside table, beside the bathtub, in the kitchen." She shook her head. "I may have a little problem."

"It makes my book collection look rather paltry by comparison."

"Ha! I don't have first editions of Jane Austen." She picked up her digital reading device. "And then there's all the books I have in here."

Charles moved closer, looking both baffled and intrigued. "There are books in there?"

"An entire library's worth." She handed the reading device to him. "We have digital books now, too. I can hop on a plane and take a dozen titles with me without taking up room in my suitcase."

He looked skeptical as he held up the device. "Can anything replace the feel of an actual book in your hand?"

"Believe me," she said fervently, "it's real. Digital or paper, a book's a book."

"I remain unconvinced."

"Fair enough." She rubbed her hands together. "I ordered a pizza, and according to the online tracker, it's out for delivery."

Charles held up his hands. "Every word out of your mouth made no sense to me."

"You've never eaten pizza?" Amber looked horrified. "That's terrible!"

"It's a food?"

"The most perfect food in the entire universe," Amber declared.

Megan retrieved plates and napkins from the galley kitchen. "It's based on a dish from Naples, Italy. Immigrants brought it to America at the end of the nineteenth century, but when GIs came back from Europe after World War II—"

"There were *two* world wars?"

She set the plates down on the coffee table. *That* was a can of worms she couldn't open right now. "I can tell you about them later. All you need to know right now is that pizza is cheesy, bready, and delicious."

"And you can *order* it…*online?*"

"I use my computer to let the pizzeria know I want it delivered to my home, and it shows up within thirty minutes."

Amber plopped down onto the sofa. "Online ordering is the best thing to happen to pizza since mozzarella cheese. It means that you don't have to talk to anybody."

"You *love* talking to people," Megan said as she arranged napkins beside the plates.

"When I'm home," Amber said, "I don't want to talk to *anybody*. It's just me, my pizza, and my binge-watching." She turned to a mystified Charles. "That's when I plant myself down in front of my television and watch it for hours, until my eyeballs turn to goo."

"How...delightful?"

"Don't knock it until you try it," Megan said. "I've been known to lose entire weekends to binging my favorite drama that features pretty people wearing pretty clothes and having pretty arguments."

Charles shook his head. "There are things about this era I will never understand."

Megan and Amber laughed.

"Wine?" Megan asked.

"Yes, please," Charles said at the same time Amber said, "Oh, yeah!"

Megan opened a bottle of sauvignon blanc that a friend from California had sent her. She poured three glasses that she handed to her guests.

"What should we toast to?" Amber asked.

"To friends," Megan said after a moment.

"May we never forget each other," Charles added. His gaze was fixed solely on her when he said it, and a whole flock of birds seemed to take flight in Megan's belly.

They clinked their glasses together. Megan sipped her wine, hoping it would ease even a little of the emotion that threatened to overwhelm her whenever she thought about saying her last goodbye to Charles.

A knock sounded at the door.

"And there's our pizza!" Megan said, before hurrying to retrieve and pay for their food.

Moments later, the pizza box lay atop her coffee table. Like a magician performing a trick, she opened the box. "Ta-da! Pepperoni pizza!"

Charles bent over the food. He drew a deep breath and his eyes drifted shut.

"My gracious," he said in a voice filled with amazement. "That is perhaps the most delightful scent I have ever encountered."

"Wait until you taste it." Megan put slices on plates and handed them to Amber and Charles. She sat cross-legged on the floor, balancing her plate in her lap. Charles sat in an armchair nearby.

She noticed Charles eyeing the pizza warily.

"Don't like mushrooms and onions?"

"I hate to be rude, but…" He cleared his throat. "You have failed to provide cutlery."

Amber gawked at him. "Friends don't let friends eat pizza with a knife and fork."

"Just pick it up with your hands," Megan said. "Like this." She demonstrated by hefting her slice and taking a big bite. She savored the flavors of tangy tomato and sweet onion, accompanied by the pepperoni and the gooey cheese. Delicious. "As usual, Lucca's Pizza has come through."

Charles gaped at her. "Sandwiches are one thing,

but certainly my mother would have had a paroxysm if she'd seen me eat with my hands."

"She'd bend the rules for pizza," Megan said. "Trust me." She eyed the pie. "Go on. Give it a try."

Warily, as though he was about to pick up a snake, Charles lifted his slice. He shot Megan an unconvinced look. She gave him an encouraging smile.

He bit into the pizza.

His eyes went wide.

"Why," he said after chewing and swallowing, "would anyone eat anything else?"

Amber and Megan laughed.

"We ask ourselves the same question," Megan said.

"Forgive me," he said. "I know it's polite to make conversation during a meal, but I simply cannot keep myself from devouring this pizza."

"Join the club." Amber chuckled.

No words were spoken as the three of them polished off an entire large pepperoni pizza in record time. Finally, when the last slice had been annihilated, everyone sat back with a happy sigh and sipped at their wine.

"So," Megan asked, turning to Amber, "are you ready to become a Broadway star?"

"I may need a little more to drink before that." Amber got up to pour herself another glass. "But not too much," she said, carefully pouring herself just a few fingers of wine. "A tipsy audition won't win me the part."

After she returned to the living room, she handed

Megan her book of monologues. One of the pages had been dog-eared.

"That's the one I'm doing," she said. "It's from a lesser-known Off Broadway play."

"Good idea not to do something too familiar." Megan flipped open the book to the correct page. "Keeps things fresh for the casting people."

"What do you need from us?" Charles asked, bracing his forearms on his knees.

"I'm going to run through it a few times, and if you see something that needs work, let me know."

Charles looked doubtful. "I have almost no knowledge of acting. Your performance the other night was my first theatrical experience."

"That makes you an even better judge," Amber said. "Nothing to compare me to, just your own feelings." She looked at Megan. "Can you be on book for me? Let me know if I bobble my lines?"

"Sure." Megan glanced over the monologue. It was about a woman confronting her absent mother, and the struggles she faced learning how to stand on her own. Even simply reading it brought tears to Megan's eyes. "This looks great. You'll completely kill it."

Amber took one sip of her wine before setting it down. She stayed on her feet and paced back and forth a few times, all the while she shook out her arms and did a few vocal exercises. After clearing her throat, she nodded at Megan and Charles.

"'You don't get to tell me how to live my life,'" she began.

Megan found herself transfixed. Amber *became* Jodie, the woman facing her negligent mother. Megan felt the depth of Jodie's anger, her sadness, and her desperate longing for a mother's love. But instead of screaming to the heavens and violently weeping, Amber kept her performance restrained, the feelings pulsing just beneath the surface. That was much more effective than going over the top with her emotions.

"'The time for me to walk away is now,'" Amber continued. "'And I won't look back.'"

Only when Amber looked at Megan and Charles expectantly did Megan realize the monologue was over. She left the book in her lap and applauded.

"That was unbelievable." Megan rubbed the back of her hand across her watering eyes. "You totally had me."

"Again," Charles said in a hushed tone, "I am in awe of your talent."

"I was worried that that long pause in the middle was going to completely undermine the momentum," Amber said.

"It didn't. It made everything all the more gut-wrenching." Megan still vibrated with the resonance of Amber's performance. She scanned the monologue book. "But it looks like you forgot the line, 'You were my first heartbreak.'"

Amber grimaced. "Darn. That's an important line."

"Want to do it again?" Megan asked. "If you're not worried about burning yourself out."

"Yeah, let's take it from the top." Amber glanced at Megan and Charles. "This isn't too boring?"

"This is the polar opposite of boring," Charles said firmly. "And as someone who's sorted a pile of screws, I consider myself an expert on what constitutes boring."

Amber laughed. "Fair enough. Here we go."

In the end, Amber did the monologue two more times before she was satisfied with it. Megan and Charles offered small suggestions, such as when to look up toward the sky, or adjusting the movement of Amber's hands. Yet these were minor alterations. Amber's acting instincts were spot-on.

By the time Amber gave her last line for the third time, Megan felt as though she'd been put through the emotional wringer.

"I don't know how you find the energy to do this over and over," Megan said, resisting the impulse to sprawl on the carpet.

"It's like exercising," Amber said. "You build up muscle strength." She eyed Charles. "I bet you can relate."

"I always had strength for working on my inventions for hours," he said, "but after the first time I took a meeting with potential investors, I wanted to crawl under my bed and stay there for a week whilst I hibernated."

"It got better, though?" Megan asked.

"Eventually, I wore *them* out. They'd say they'd invest their money so long as I let them go home." He grinned. "An effective strategy."

Megan smiled but said to Amber, "We should get this on tape so we have time to edit and upload everything."

"Good idea," Amber said. "I borrowed a lavalier microphone from the theater department so that the audio quality is as crisp and professional as possible." She tilted her head at Charles. "You know what a microphone is?"

He lifted a brow. "By my time, they had been in existence for over thirty years. I'm not *completely* old-fashioned." Yet he undercut his haughty words with a chuckle.

It took about twenty minutes of positioning the camera, fitting Amber with the mike, and doing tests before she was satisfied with the technical setup. Megan was appointed camera operator while Charles stood at the ready with the monologue's text, on the off chance that Amber might flub a line.

In the end, Amber recorded the monologue twice, just in case. They all reviewed the footage on her laptop, with Charles shaking his head in wonder at the ease and speed of recording a moving image with sound.

"This puts the Lumière brothers' cinematograph and Edison's kinetoscope to shame," he said with an awed shake of his head. "Any chance I can take your computing device back to 1902 with me? I could quadruple my fortune."

"Nope," Amber said and laughed.

Megan's smile felt strained and tight. She'd almost

forgotten that tomorrow night, Charles would return to his time. But clearly he hadn't.

It'll be over soon. I can get on with my regularly-scheduled programming, and this will all fade away.

Yet it wouldn't fade. The pain might dull a bit, but for the rest of her life, she'd know that the man who'd won her heart was far away, and that she'd never see him again.

She made herself concentrate on the here and now. There was Amber's audition video to edit, and a celebration with her friends afterward. And tomorrow was Christmas Eve. The holiday always cheered her. Hopefully, it would again.

Amber knew the editing software best, but she took Megan and Charles's suggestions when it came to cutting the piece to its best advantage. Finally, they arrived at a finished product that satisfied Amber.

"Quick," she said to Megan, "before I change my mind, can I get your WiFi password so I can send it?"

"Again," Charles said, "you speak words that are incomprehensible to me."

"It's nothing you need to worry about," Megan said. "There's no internet in 1902." She wrote down the password on an index card and gave it to Amber, who quickly got to work composing an email.

"Yes. Quite." Charles's words were clipped, his expression closed off, and she realized that she'd been pretty rude.

"I'm sorry," she said to Charles, hating that she'd hurt him at all. "I sounded like a total witch. It's just that…" She exhaled. "I'm going to miss you."

Miss barely covered how deeply his absence would hurt her. What she felt for him was so much stronger than friendship, even deeper than something as insubstantial as a crush. She thought about him first thing in the morning, he occupied her mind all day, and he filled her awareness when she got into bed at night.

I think I...

Oh, no.

She'd done it. Gone and fallen in love with him. Of all the terrible things she could have done, this was the worst. Because he didn't love her back, and within twenty-four hours, he'd be gone forever.

"There!" Amber stepped back from her computer. "I've sent it."

"Congratulations!" Megan hugged her.

"I couldn't have done this without your encouragement and help." Amber glanced back and forth between Megan and Charles. "Both of you."

"It was an honor," Charles said, smiling.

How could Megan feel so happy and yet so devastated at the same time?

She took her empty glass and bottle of wine into the kitchen and poured herself more to drink. As she took a sip, she realized the futility of trying to dull her emotions with alcohol. Nothing would make her feelings go away—except time, and even then, they wouldn't disappear entirely. They would be like a scar that faded but never fully vanished. She'd remember the wound for the rest of her life.

CHAPTER SIXTEEN

Charles rolled over and turned on the bedside lamp. It no longer amazed him that electricity was so commonplace, or that the lights it powered were so bright.

Strange how, though he still struggled with things such as the pace of life or the vast amount of information, he'd also quickly adapted to this new world. Much of the ease of his transition was because of Megan's patience and kindness.

He glanced down at the Whitley-Moran Mansion souvenir T-shirt he now wore, and grimaced. The very fact that Harold Moran's name was tacked onto Charles's was insupportable. Nothing that belonged to Charles ought to be in that knave's possession—including Eliza. Though Eliza didn't *belong* to anyone except herself. Nobody was another person's possession.

Still, it stuck in Charles's craw that Moran had everything Charles had wanted. Charles had to return to 1902, if for no other reason than to show up the snob.

Tomorrow night…he'd be back home again. The world of the twenty-first century would be gone. All its innovations and wonders. All of its people.

Guilt jabbed him because, after Amber had submitted her audition video, he hadn't joined the celebration for Megan. Staying away was the sensible thing to do, however. The more time he spent with everyone here in the future—especially Megan—the more difficult it would be to return home.

So Megan had dropped him off at the mansion while she and Amber had continued on to Tina's Diner for the much-vaunted peppermint cheesecake. Charles had been acutely aware of how alone he was then, waving goodbye to them as Megan's car drove off, and then turning and walking on his solitary path back to the house.

He'd never felt quite as isolated as he had then, letting himself into the deserted mansion and venturing to the modernized wing. It was difficult not to picture everybody celebrating—without him.

Dan had a name for that peculiar sensation. *FOMO*, he called it. *Fear Of Missing Out*. Charles had that sensation in spades.

So he'd showered and gotten into bed with a novel Megan had loaned him from her own collection. It was a romance set about twenty years before his time in the Arizona territory. Charles had stayed up far too late reading about the characters' road to a happily ever after.

Eventually, he forced himself to put the book aside and try sleeping.

That had been a complete failure. He'd lain awake for an hour.

Charles got out of bed. He contemplated reading more of the novel, but he'd surely stay up until dawn in an attempt to finish it before it was time for him to go. He'd taken care of most of the components for his project for Megan, and the rest had to be assembled outside.

Rather than work on the project or finish the book, he went to the television set, but turned it off immediately after turning it on. Watching things passively held no appeal for him tonight. He needed to move.

The bag of borrowed clothing held plenty of warm garments, so he quickly dressed in many layers. After pulling on his coat and wrapping a muffler around his neck, he jogged downstairs. There was a side entrance he planned to make use of.

He went to the door as quickly as he could. In his pocket was the spare key to the mansion, as well as the code for the security system.

Charles chuckled to himself as he punched in the numbers on the keypad. He certainly *had* adapted to this new environment if something like an electronic alarm system didn't even make him blink.

He stepped outside. The night was cold and dark,

his breath misting in front of his face as he looked up at the swath of stars that sparkled overhead.

When had he last looked at the stars? When had been the last time he'd done anything for the pure pleasure of experiencing life, instead of trying to get from one point to another?

A memory rose to his mind: sitting in the theater with Megan as he'd been swept up in the drama and comedy of the holiday plays. And later that same night, when he and Megan had twirled Hula-Hoops in the Turners' backyard.

Both recollections made him smile.

Still, the urge to be in motion pushed at him. Megan had programmed a taxi cab company number into his telephone, so he knew that if he needed a ride somewhere, it was available—though he was still strapped for cash. The lack of money wasn't a problem. What he needed right now was the feel of the earth beneath his feet.

He walked down the house's long driveway until he came to the main road leading into Cutter Springs, then headed toward town. The gravel crunched beneath his feet, and the nearly-full moon illuminated the ribbon of road. The air smelled crisp, scented with pine from the trees lining the highway. It was quiet as there were no other houses along the road, and most animals were sensibly asleep in their nests or dens.

Long ago, even before his parents' death, he'd been apt to go for late-night rambles. Being out by himself as the rest of the world slept helped settle his active mind. He would walk through the scrubby forest that surrounded his childhood home, twigs snapping beneath his boots. Later on, when he'd lived in the boarding house in town, he'd amble up and down the streets and look into the darkened shop windows, planning for a time when he no longer lived hand to mouth.

So it was familiar to be out as he was now, and he welcomed the feeling of the nighttime spreading all around him. As he walked, an occasional automobile passed him, heading who knew where at this late hour. Perhaps those drivers had the same impulse to be out in the small hours. Or perhaps they were heading places on their own journeys.

One of the vehicles passed him, then stopped and backed up until he and the automobile were beside each other. It was a vehicle that Megan had called a *pickup*. The driver lowered the window, revealing a man with a well-groomed, coppery beard.

"You okay?" the man asked. "Did your car break down?"

"Just out for an evening constitutional," Charles said.

"It's two o'clock in the morning," the man noted.

"A morning constitutional, then."

The man looked uncertain. "Need a lift?"

Charles considered it. The walk felt good, as it always had, but a talk with a friendly stranger held its own appeal.

"If you wouldn't mind dropping me in town…?"

Before returning to his era, he could walk through Cutter Springs as he had walked through the mill town of his adolescence. Granted, he was a man now, and not something midway between a boy and an adult, but he could adjust to the difference.

"Nothing's open right now," the man said. His brow cleared. "Oh, there's the twenty-four-hour doughnut shop."

"That sounds like an excellent destination."

"Get in." The man nodded to the seat beside him.

Charles walked around the pickup and opened the door. A gust of warm air wafted out, making him realize just how cold he'd gotten. Gratefully, he climbed into the passenger seat and fastened his seat belt. Two voices, a man's and a woman's, murmured in the radio broadcast.

"I'm Ali," the driver said as they pulled back onto the road.

"Charles. Pleasure to meet you."

"You usually take walks at two a.m., Charles?"

"On occasion," he said to Ali. "I just wanted to feel the road beneath me."

"I hear you," Ali said. "I live with my sister and her husband and kids in a house that's not really big enough for all of us. When I get antsy, I usually go for a drive."

"At the moment, I have no means of transportation. Other than on foot or relying on kind strangers," he added with a smile. "Where are you headed at this hour? One of those late-night drives?"

"I'm headed to work at the postal processing center." He nodded down at the emblem on his coat with its image of an eagle. "Let me tell you, we sure are busy this time of year. So many cards, and packages, and gifts." He whistled. "But it's not so bad. We know we're making people happy."

"That is a valuable service." A car passed them, heading in the opposite direction. Its lights briefly illuminated the interior of the pickup, and Charles could see some of the weariness that formed shadows beneath Ali's eyes.

"What do you do, Charles?"

A corner of Charles's mouth twitched. "Currently, I impersonate myself."

Ali glanced over at him, and the look on his face clearly indicated that he wasn't certain if his passenger was altogether sane.

"That is, I'm a historical reenactor," Charles said quickly, using the term that Megan and Phillip had taught him. "At the mansion."

"Oh, yeah! My nephew has been dying to visit."

"You should come with your family. There's a party on Christmas Eve that's open to the public. I promise it will be worthwhile."

Ali frowned. "Didn't the guy who owned that place vanish, like, *poof*, over a century ago?"

How strange to hear of himself referred to in that way, including his disappearance. But Charles couldn't explain to Ali exactly what had happened to him.

Instead, he said, "He did. But I have it on good

authority that he would welcome you and your family into his home."

"Maybe we will stop by tonight."

"Excellent." Charles hoped that Ali would come. The idea of opening his home to this kind man and his relations filled him with happiness.

"You do anything else besides work at the mansion?" Ali asked.

"My main line of work is in steel." That was close to the truth, anyway.

"Right! There's a mill between Cutter Springs and Bellville, one town over. Moran Steel."

Charles ground his teeth together as anger tightened his muscles. So, Moran had taken over Charles's Bellville mill, too. *The rogue.*

"They usually have a big Christmas party for the workers," Ali said. "They take over the Belham Hotel ballroom. I heard it's an old tradition, dating all the way back to the mill's original owner—that Whitley guy who disappeared. There's a big buffet and dancing. Stockings full of presents for the kids."

Pleasure spread warmly through Charles's chest. Was the continuation of the party Eliza's doing, or was it…possibly…Moran's?

Might it be that Charles's rival wasn't entirely a scoundrel?

"It's supposed to be pretty amazing," Ali continued. "I guess Whitley was known for his generosity."

"Is that so?" Charles felt his face grow far warmer than the heater in the automobile might be responsible for. Very peculiar to hear himself praised for behavior he considered ordinary—expected, even. If a man accrued a fortune through the labor of others, it was only right that he would treat those others with respect and honor. He hadn't gotten to his position of wealth and power without many hands' contribution.

Giving back to his employees wasn't praiseworthy. It just made sense.

Lights and buildings increased as the forest gave way to town. Soon, they were nearing the downtown area. Though the streets were empty, the shine of tinsel and holiday lights reflected in the wet streets. He and Ali passed the town's enormous Christmas tree, sparkling in the depths of night. Charles once again admired Lydia Romano's work in its decoration, both cheerful and elegant, as well as Sophia's star at the very top.

The smile on his lips faded as he realized he'd never get to see little Sophia grow up. He wouldn't see her take the world by storm with her intelligence and curiosity. All Charles could do was wish the best for her.

He tried to distract himself from these glum thoughts by looking at the slumbering town. Had he possessed the time, he would have enjoyed exploring present-day Cutter Springs. There were restaurants and shops and an art gallery, not to mention the library he'd visited briefly. There was also something that called itself a Virtual Reality Arcade, which sounded vaguely sinister. The town had certainly grown and changed since his time, though Megan had showed him a small glimpse back into the past.

Cutter Springs looked like a grand place to raise a family. Hopefully, it would be the same back in his time.

They passed Tina's Diner, which was closed. Not far from the restaurant, Ali pulled up next to a small café with an illuminated sign advertising DONUTS AND LATTES. HERE OR TO GO. Several large vehicles were parked outside. The window showed a few men seated at tables, steaming cups set in front of them. Rather than looking desolate at this late hour, the café seemed cheerful and welcoming, exactly the sort of place that might welcome a restless wanderer in the middle of the night.

"Here we are," Ali said. "Be sure to get the buttermilk maple cruller. It's killer."

"Will you join me?"

"Wish I could, but I'm due at the sorting center in twenty minutes."

"Perhaps I can treat you to something to go?" he asked. "Some coffee and one of those *killer* buttermilk maple crullers?" Charles remembered seeing people carrying steaming paper cups that were almost as ever-present as mobile telephones. It seemed that people of this era were in desperate need to hold things in their hands.

Ali thought about it for a moment. "I could use the sugar and caffeine."

"Then it's settled."

235

He and Ali entered the café together, the bell on the door chiming merrily as they came inside. At once, Charles was surrounded by the wonderful scents of coffee and fried dough. The walls were painted a jaunty pink, and they were hung with chocolate-brown framed pictures of doughnuts. The counter occupied one room, and the sitting area held café tables and mismatched chairs. The customers at their tables gave friendly waves to him and Ali.

"Hey, Ali," a man with a blond beard said.

"Hi, Ed," Ali answered. "Keeping warm?"

"Trying to!"

"Happy holidays," the blonde woman behind the counter said cheerfully. She wore a red-and-white velvet Santa Claus hat. "What can I get you two gentlemen?"

"Two buttermilk maple crullers, please," Charles said. "One to go, one for here. Coffee for me. And what would you care to drink, Ali?"

"The biggest, most caffeinated thing you've got," the other man said readily.

"One Ultra Chai Triple Espresso coming up." The woman busied herself with a large, brass machine that hissed and steamed. It put the Corliss steam engine to shame, and looked equally as complex to operate.

A few moments later, a paper cup that looked like a water tank was set on the counter in front of Ali, along with a paper bag holding the much-celebrated cruller. Charles's coffee appeared in a ceramic mug, and a doughnut on a bright-pink plate.

"What do I owe you?" Charles asked.

The woman nodded at the emblem on Ali's coat. "For a postal worker on Christmas Eve, it's free. Same for your friend."

"Thanks!" Ali said, smiling.

"Without you," the woman said, "Santa would have a lot more work to do."

"Much appreciated," Charles said. He turned to Ali. "Thank you for the ride and the company. Oh—and the doughnut and coffee."

"Glad to lend a hand. 'Tis the season, and all that." Ali headed toward the door, but paused. "See you at the Christmas party?"

"I'll be there."

Ali gave him a small salute before heading outside. A few moments later, he drove off toward his place of employment, ensuring that Christmas gifts could be put beneath trees, and many happy memories would be made.

Charles took a seat at an empty table. Customers at other tables talked in low, early morning voices, creating a pleasant background sound as he looked out the window at the quiet town. Garlands of electrical lights were hung along buildings and wrapped around lampposts, looking like constellations. It was peaceful and pretty, and hardly any of it would exist when he returned to his era.

Perhaps, when he did go back to 1902, he could be more involved in developing Cutter Springs's holiday festivities. They could have a tree-lighting ceremony too, and carolers that walked through town. And sleigh rides for children, with bells on the horses so that they made a musical, jolly sound as they walked. Yes, that would be quite nice.

He looked down into his coffee cup with a dry smile. This past week in the twenty-first century had certainly altered him if he was thinking of sleigh rides and carolers rather than business strategies and technological innovation.

What would people think of him when he went back? Would they be suspicious of his changes, or would they embrace them?

Rosie would certainly be shocked. He smiled to think of his take-charge housekeeper, and the modern woman she'd inspired.

His smile faded as he thought of Megan, who played Rosie with such zest. When he said goodbye to Megan in less than twenty-four hours, it would be a true farewell. They'd never see each other again.

It was too raw, too painful, to think of that. It made his chest ache.

He sighed heavily—but it didn't make the hurt go away.

When he returned, he'd spend more time with Eliza. He would come to know her better. They were engaged, and yet he'd never let her get close, so much so that they barely had a relationship.

What were Eliza's favorite foods? He knew Megan ate the delicious soup called *pho*, and she'd introduced him to the magnificence of pizza.

Did Eliza have a particular passion? He didn't know. But he did know that Megan loved romance novels, and history, and showing people of the modern era the importance and wonder of the past.

After a year's acquaintance, half a year of courting, and three months' engagement, he knew almost nothing about Eliza.

Things would be different upon his return. He would take the time to get to know her, learn her loves and dislikes, what drove her, what she hoped for, and what she feared. He would be a better man, a better fiancé, and one day, a better husband and father.

Hopefully, she'd also like the improved Charles Whitley. *He* rather liked the improved Charles Whitley. He wasn't perfect by any stretch of the imagination, but he was certainly different.

The lunar eclipse was almost here. The hands of the clock would turn once more, and then this place and these people would be gone, existing only in his memory and in the future.

There was more work to be done between now and then, which was good. Staying busy was important.

It would keep his mind off things he didn't want to consider...including never seeing Megan again.

CHAPTER SEVENTEEN

Megan rubbed her weary eyes as she headed toward the staff room. Last night had run very late, which, combined with a full workday, made her drag this morning.

Tina had been forced to gently but firmly escort her, Dan, Amber, and Phillip out the door of her diner at eleven. They'd polished off an entire peppermint cheesecake in between toasting her and Amber with mugs of hot chocolate. Fun as the celebration had been, there had been a hole left by Charles's absence. As if by mutual agreement, no one spoke of it, or the fact that he'd soon be returning to 1902, but that didn't make his absence any easier to take.

Once Megan had returned home, she'd stayed up even later taking care of two very important tasks. The first was submitting her finalized application for the teaching position at the university. The second project was in her hand right now in the form of a gift bag.

She felt a little like she was handling a live bomb. It might detonate, or it might not.

Hopefully, there would be no devastating explosions today.

She'd reached a decision sometime around two o'clock in the morning. It was odd, she was never awake at that hour, but she was this morning. She'd had the strangest sensation of feeling particularly connected to Charles at that moment. It was silly, because he was no doubt asleep. Yet she'd been huddled on her couch and had sensed his nearby presence, so strongly that she felt she could almost reach out and touch him.

You couldn't be haunted by someone if they weren't a ghost, could you?

But as she'd been wrapped in her favorite afghan, crocheted by her grandmother, understanding had hit her like a beam of sunlight breaking through the clouds.

She had to tell Charles how she felt about him. She needed to be honest with him and with herself, before it was too late. If after hearing her pour her heart out to him he still wanted to leave, then she'd accept it, understanding that she had done everything she could. But if she kept quiet, she'd be withholding the truth and denying them both a chance to be happy.

If anything, his time with her had taught her the value of speaking up and taking chances. Nothing would happen if she stayed still, if she kept herself safe. She had to take the chance.

This risk scared the heck out of her, and that told

her she had to take it. The bigger the risk, the bigger the possible reward.

And the bigger the hurt if I fail.

She pushed that thought out of her head. Doubting herself would derail her.

"Have you seen Charles?" she asked as she entered the staff room. Amber hadn't arrived, but Dan was there, a pen in his hand as he tried to solve a sudoku puzzle.

The museum would be open in an hour and she wanted to take advantage of the brief lull to talk with Charles. Thinking about what she had to say made her palms damp and her mouth dry.

Nervously, she shifted the gift bag she held from one hand to the other.

Dan looked up from his puzzle. "I think he went outside. He mentioned something about the gazebo."

"Thanks." She turned to go.

"Hey, Megan?"

She turned back to Dan. "Yes?"

"I just wanted to say that no matter what happens tonight, you've done a lot for Charles, and yourself. It takes a lot of guts to put yourself out there."

A lump formed in Megan's throat. "Thank you."

Dan's mouth hitched into a smile. "Remember how I said that I was working at a coffee shop when I met Lydia?"

Megan nodded.

"Took me three whole months of serving Lydia her

latte before I could even say hello, let alone ask her on a date."

"But you did," Megan noted.

"I did, even though I thought I would pass out and they'd have to call an ambulance. Fortunately, she said yes. It turned out that she'd wanted to ask me on a date, too, but she was also shy."

"And now you're married," Megan said, "and have Sophia."

"I got the happily ever after. But it wasn't easy."

She glanced down at the gift bag. Hopefully, its contents would reveal everything she felt, but if it didn't, she had to be prepared and truly stick her neck out.

I can do this. I got the letter of recommendation, and I can do this, too.

"I'm about to take a chance," she said to Dan. "It might go well, it might be a disaster."

"You're trying, though," he said with an uplifted finger, "and that's what matters."

Emotion made her throat ache. She crossed the staff room and gave him a quick hug. "Thanks."

"Always my pleasure," he said as he hugged her back.

She moved away, and her heart began to pound. There was no putting it off any longer. "Okay...well, wish me luck."

"You don't need luck," Dan said with a kind smile. "You've got yourself, and that's enough."

Dan's words touched her deeply, all the way to a vulnerable place that she'd tried so hard to protect.

She blinked her eyes furiously to hold back a trickle of tears. She couldn't fall apart now. Maybe later, she'd allow herself to give in and just let her feelings swamp her. For now, she had to keep moving forward.

After breathing in and out slowly, she left the staff room and headed down the hallway. As she walked, she took in again the bright and cheerful holiday decorations that warmed the mansion. The giant house's rooms were always splendid, but the Christmas adornments softened what was often an imposing, stately building.

And with Charles living there, it felt far more like a home and less like a museum. Granted, he was just one man, and he was restricted to living in the modern section of the mansion, but the house belonged to him. He *inhabited* it. She'd always loved coming to work, but knowing he'd be here made her drive all the faster each morning.

It's not the atmosphere of the house that makes me hurry here every day. She recognized that now.

She reached the door that led to the sweeping meadow beside the house. Snow blanketed the grass and the paths, making everything shimmer and sparkle beneath the morning sunlight.

A set of footprints showed Charles's route, and she followed them until the gazebo rose up before her. Phillip had arranged to have it decorated for the holiday. There were more evergreen swags and shiny ornaments around the posts, and hanging from the roof.

While these things were lovely, they didn't snare her attention the way a man's solitary figure did, standing at one railing and looking out at the woods.

Megan's heart kicked like a rabbit, but she made herself keep walking. She could do this. If it went badly, she could live with the consequences, but she had to give it a try.

"Merry Christmas Eve Day," she said, climbing the steps of the gazebo.

Charles turned to face her as she approached, his expression warm, making her feel like there were hundreds of pinwheels spinning inside her.

"And a Merry Christmas Eve Day to you."

She neared, torn between wanting to run to him and the urge to take off in the opposite direction. Together, they stood at the railing to gaze at the trees.

"I almost never came out here," he said softly. "There was so much I had built here—gardens, fountains, a greenhouse—and yet I didn't enjoy them."

She swallowed, hearing the melancholy in his voice. "And now?"

"Now..." He exhaled. "I'm going to take more time. I'm going to look around me and appreciate everything that I have. I've truly come to appreciate what I believed I hadn't time to enjoy—such as the holiday season, and letting people in." He turned to her. "Because of you."

Her pulse stuttered at the same time that happiness

spread in a golden wave through her. Maybe there was hope for her, after all.

"I'm glad I could give you that," she said sincerely. "And *you* helped me realize that if there's something I want, I should go out and get it."

Now.

"To that end, I need to tell you something."

She faced him. Somehow, she managed to keep standing, even though it seemed like the wooden floor of the gazebo pitched beneath her.

"Charles, I'm falling in love with you. Would you be willing to stay here, in this time, with me?"

There. I've said it. And the world didn't end.

She searched his face for a reaction, dreading and hoping at the same time. His eyes were full of affection—and sadness.

That's not what I want to see.

"Oh, Megan." He sighed. "I also have feelings for you."

Giddiness rose up. And yet she could sense the *but* in his voice and in his gaze. She tamped down her joy, telling it to wait before bursting out.

"Yet..." Desolation gleamed in the blue of his eyes. "I need to go back to 1902." He shook his head as if the movement caused him physical pain. "I'm a man from a different era."

That was *not* what she wanted to hear. She felt herself frantically grabbing at empty air, yet there was nothing to hold on to.

"You've already learned so much about this one in

such a short time," she said. "It wouldn't take long to get the hang of things."

"Perhaps not." He looked away, toward the sparkling snow.

"I'm still hearing a *however*," she said sadly.

His expression darkened. "I cannot let Harold Moran win," he said tightly. His jaw firmed. "Letting him have everything that was supposed to be mine is unacceptable. I must return and claim my life."

It hurt badly that she wasn't enough to keep him here, and that he considered the life they could have together to be of less worth than taking back something from his past.

She felt like a balloon the day after a birthday party. All the happiness was gone, leaving her limp and deflated. A flare of anger rose up, that maybe he valued getting the best of his nemesis over her and Charles's possible happiness.

"So, you're pushing away love and going back... for spite."

"It's not like that," he said, his words low.

"Then what is it like?" A note of heated frustration sounded in her voice.

Ridges appeared in his brow. "With my time here, I've learned to be a different person. Maybe a better one. And I need to see what that different, better me does with my life in my own century. If I don't, I'll always wonder, 'What if?'"

Megan dipped her head, heavy with understanding. "I...I see."

She had to let him go. She couldn't be a shackle around him, chaining him in place. Supporting his choice was the right path to walk—painful as it was.

But there was one thing left for her to do before she could retreat and lick her wounds.

She cleared her throat. "I have something for you." She held out the gift bag.

"What is it?"

"A little Christmas gift. That is," she added wryly, "if you don't mind Christmas gifts."

Smile lines fanned out from the corners of his eyes. "I don't anymore, especially if they're from you. Thank you," he said sincerely, taking the present from her.

"Don't open it until Christmas Day in 1902." She wouldn't get to see him open it.

His face fell. "I have something for you, too—but I doubt it's as special as this."

"I'm sure it is." Her throat felt like a boa constrictor was wrapped around it, yet she could eke out a few words. "And no matter what, you've given me a tremendous gift, one I'll treasure always."

He reached out and took her hand. She wore gloves and so did he, but the feeling of his fingers weaving with hers struck her right down to her bones. It felt so comfortable, so right, as if she had been looking for home and had finally found it.

Even though it couldn't last, she'd remember this sensation for the rest of her days.

Together, hand in hand, they stood at the railing,

looking at the woods and feeling time inevitably slipping forward.

"Okay, people," Phillip said to the staff after the morning tour had finished. "The big Christmas Eve party is tonight, and I'm bringing in Tina's catering crew and extra staff to set up. So I want you all to go home and take a break before this evening."

"Are you sure we can't help?" Dan asked.

Phillip shook his head. "Nope. Just rest up, and come prepared to have a good time tonight."

Megan glanced at Charles. She had the frantic urge to cram in as many experiences with him as possible before he was gone. Maybe there would be time for them to go see a movie matinee, or even just head to the library and play a game of silent tag.

But Charles hurried over to Phillip, and in a moment, they were deep in conversation.

It was probably better to spend less time with Charles. Maybe it would make his leaving a little easier to bear.

"Want to get a cup of coffee?" she asked Amber.

The other woman offered her an apologetic smile. "I don't think I'm up for conversation. My big plan is to go home and stew about the audition." She grimaced. "I can't believe I did it."

"But you did, and you were great," Megan said with conviction. "When do you find out about the part?"

"I'm not sure. They want to cast quickly, since the

production is scheduled to go up in the early spring. Soon, maybe?" Amber wrinkled her nose in worry. "I don't know how I can live with the waiting."

"I completely understand." Megan let out a shaky breath. "Last night, I sent my application in for the teaching position."

Amber's eyes went round. "Oh, my gosh! That's great!"

"So we're in the same boat." Megan gave a wry chuckle. "It's a pretty rocky boat, and I may get seasick."

"You know what they say about fighting seasickness," Amber said. "Keep your eyes on the horizon."

"I understand." Besides fretting about her teaching application, Megan was a bundle of nerves about tonight. Her limbs felt jittery and unsteady. The mansion's party was always something she enjoyed, but it wasn't enough to distract her from Charles's return home. "Will you make it tonight?"

"I can't miss it, or else Phillip will sulk."

Megan chuckled. "He totally will."

"Besides," Amber added, "the party is always great and I have a feeling you might need a friend…" Her gaze softened. "…you know, after."

Megan's chest squeezed tightly. Those moments after Charles's departure would surely be the hardest. Amber seemed to know this, and while her consideration didn't lessen the pain, it made it a little easier to bear. Hopefully, Amber wouldn't mind seeing Megan ugly cry.

It was a strange thing to anticipate sobbing with

a broken heart, like she was baking and decorating a cake with the sole intention of dropping it on the ground without taking a single bite.

"See you tonight, then," Megan said.

After shouldering her bag, Amber gave Megan a quick hug. "If you can, try not to sit and brood about it. Maybe lose yourself in the fact that it's Christmas Eve."

"I'll try."

With a nod, Amber headed out.

Megan didn't bother asking Dan if he wanted to grab coffee. He'd already said that he'd be frantically wrapping Sophia's presents while his daughter was at her grandparents'.

Still, the idea of going back to her apartment and killing time watching makeover shows wasn't appealing. It would just remind her of how alone she'd be once Charles had gone.

Which was how she found herself, thirty minutes later, at her parents' house, sitting at the breakfast bar and eating the grilled cheese sandwich and tomato soup her father had made for her. As usual, her dad had put together a delicious meal. The food reminded her of the simplicity of childhood, when a devastating loss (of, say, her favorite boy-band backpack) could be mended by the application of melted cheddar between buttery slices of bread.

"Nathan and Elena went out to do some last-minute shopping," her dad said, "and your mother's with her Meals on Wheels group, packing up Christmas dinners for seniors, so it's just us." He scratched his chin in thought. "The tree's all decorated, but we could cut up some paper snowflakes and cover the bathroom with them."

"Mm," Megan said, barely paying attention. All she could think about was that night, and saying her final goodbye to Charles.

"Or maybe we could build a huge bonfire in the front yard and burn all of our ugly Christmas sweaters while singing 'Kumbaya.'"

"Sounds good," she murmured.

"Meg-bear." Her dad put his hand on her shoulder, startling her back to awareness. "You okay?"

She tried for a smile, but didn't quite succeed. "A little tired. I was up late last night, sending in my application for the teaching job." She wouldn't tell her dad about the other thing that had kept her so busy recently, wanting to save that as something between her and Charles.

"That's great about the application!" He gave her shoulder a squeeze.

"Thanks. It's a little disconcerting, knowing that my future is being decided—maybe at this very moment."

"Whatever happens, you tried your best. That's all you can do." Her dad looked intently at her face. "I see the dark circles, and I also see the sadness in your eyes. That's not about the application, though, right?"

"Not that, no." She listlessly picked up her sandwich. It would be a shame not to eat it because she knew it would be delicious, but her appetite was nowhere to be found, so she set the sandwich back down.

"No one should look gloomy on Christmas Eve." His brow furrowed. "Tonight's the big party at the mansion, right? That should be fun."

"It will be." She stirred her soup, still trying to win the battle over her lack of appetite. "But Charles is leaving soon."

"I see." Her father frowned. "Your mother and I talked about your feelings for him. Does he know that you care?"

"He does." The sadness in her felt heavier than any rain cloud, and she had little hope that the sun would come out for a very long time. "It's not enough to make him stay."

"Oh, Meg-bear. If he can't see how amazing you are, then it's his loss, not yours."

Her dad hugged her, and she felt her eyes grow hot and scratchy. Thank goodness for daddies, there to wipe their daughters' noses and tell them everything was going to be all right, and then take those daughters out for ice cream.

"It's okay," she said, and sniffed. "I'm happy I went after what I wanted, even if it didn't give me the results I wanted."

"Know what will make you feel better?"

She smiled, already knowing the answer.

"Ice cream," they said in unison.

Her dad wheeled to the freezer and opened it. "Let's

see…we've got cookies 'n cream, strawberry, and… ooh, mint chocolate chip." He held up the container with a triumphant smile.

There was only one true answer.

"Mint chocolate chip, please."

As he got out two bowls and spoons, Megan hopped down from her stool to get the ice cream scoop. She could do this. She could move on with her life, a little damaged, a little hurt, but stronger for having lived through and survived the experience. Heck, history was full of stories of people who had triumphed over the toughest of circumstances. Ida B. Wells survived the early loss of her parents and a sibling, going on to become an important journalist and activist.

Megan could take comfort in that. A loss like this one would be painful, but it wouldn't be the end.

Her phone rang, and she moved to send it to voicemail, then she saw the name on the screen. She answered the call so fast, she jammed her finger.

"Hi, Doctor Hayes," she said, greeting the head of the university's history department.

Her dad sent her a questioning look, and she gave him a baffled shrug.

"Hello, Megan," Doctor Hayes said in her jovial voice. "I hope I'm not disturbing you in the middle of any Christmas Eve celebrations."

"No, no, just having some ice cream with my dad."

"Mint chocolate chip, I hope!"

"You know it." She cleared her throat. This was either very bad, or very good. "How can I help you?"

"We were all very excited to see your application for the teaching position finally come in. Some members of the faculty were beginning to think you didn't want to come work for us."

Her heart sank. "Oh, no—"

"But when your application showed up, along with all the necessary transcripts and letters of recommendation, we knew we had to act fast." The sounds of typing could be heard in the background. "I know it's a little last minute, but can you come in next week to interview?"

"Um, I…" Megan couldn't believe it. This was really happening. "Yes! Yes," she said with a bit more calm. "I would love that."

"Perfect." There were more typing sounds. "I'll have my administrative assistant call you on Monday to set up a day and time. Sound good?"

"Sounds great!" Her pulse was pounding harder than the Little Drummer Boy's drum. She flashed her dad the thumbs-up sign. "Merry Christmas!"

"Merry Christmas, Megan." With that, Doctor Hayes ended the call.

"Everything okay?" her dad asked, coming up beside her.

She turned to him, dazed. "Everything is amazing. That was the head of the university's history department. They want me to come in next week and interview for the teaching position."

"Meg-bear! That's wonderful!" He hugged her again, squeezing her tightly. "Now we definitely deserve ice cream. Oh, but first, let me text your mother. You just know she's going to brag to everyone about her daughter, the history professor." He pulled out his phone and his thumbs moved quickly across the screen.

"I don't have the job yet," Megan felt compelled to point out.

Her dad waved that away. "A mere technicality. If they called you on Christmas Eve to set up an interview, they want to hire you." He beamed at her. "Looks like you're getting your Christmas wish!"

"Looks like." She was almost dizzy with excitement over possibly landing her dream job. Yet the shadow of Charles's imminent departure continued to hang over everything, dimming her joy.

CHAPTER EIGHTEEN

It felt good for Charles to work outside in the crisp air, letting the coolness sting his face and spread through his lungs. Moving his body and staying busy kept unwanted thoughts back, and he could focus on his task rather than worry whether or not the lunar eclipse would trigger the time travel—or what the consequences would be of his going back to 1902.

Standing on the mansion's front lawn, he lifted a piece of metal, fit it into place, and used a large screwdriver to tighten it. He gave the piece a solid shake to make sure it was secure. One section down, five more to go.

"This looks very cool, but does Phillip know what you're doing?" Dan asked, walking up to survey Charles's work.

"He does," Charles answered as he rummaged through a tool bag. "He was so charmed by the idea that he lent me these tools to help me set it up. Although," he added, pulling out what appeared to be a drill powered by a battery, "a few of these are outside of my area of expertise."

Charles put the drill back into the bag. Better to stick with what he knew.

"What *is* it?" Dan walked along the construction of metal and wood that formed a frame along the front of the mansion. It resembled something akin to a scaffold, with small engines and wheels here and there, as well as unlit strings of lights that Charles had borrowed from some of the house's decorations—with Phillip's permission, of course.

"This will be a Christmas surprise." Charles used a soldering iron to affix a wire into place, which connected to one of the pieces he'd built in the staff room. Everything needed to be perfect for tonight. He needed to give Megan something before he left her forever.

"Surprise for the guests tonight?"

"Them," Charles acknowledged. "And Megan."

"Interesting," Dan said cryptically.

Charles decided not to investigate what that comment meant.

His limbs felt made of lead, to say nothing of the weight in his chest, making any movement doubly difficult. Yet he pushed himself to remain in motion, fueled by a desire to complete the task he'd given himself.

It was expected that he'd feel some melancholy just before his departure—or so he told himself. He'd worked through sadness before, especially after losing his parents. He could work through this unhappiness, too. There was shelter in work.

"I thought you were wrapping gifts for Sophia," he said.

"Lydia called me and said Sophia was done at her grandparents' and that they were spending the afternoon at home, watching Christmas movies."

Charles had seen a few of these *movies* on television—and they were a far cry from the short, black-and-white pieces he'd viewed in his own era. They appeared to be similar to plays, except with a much bigger canvas to work with. Some of them involved casts upwards of hundreds of people, and settings that defied imagination. One could perform literal magic within a movie—ride a dragon or conjure a spell or fight undead people. That last notion was much less appealing to him, but there was something for everyone.

If he remained in this era, he could learn more about movies. He could learn a great many things, like how to drive one of the amazing automobiles that came straight from an H. G. Wells novel, or which restaurant made the best pizza. Or what Megan looked like when she woke up in the morning.

Unaware of Charles's thoughts, Dan said, "I'll have to wait until Sophia goes to sleep tonight to get the wrapping done. It's not too bad—Lydia and I have a tradition of sharing spiked hot chocolate while wrestling with tape and scissors."

"I'm certain everything will be fine," Charles

said, his words sounding like they came from a great distance away.

Dan crossed his arms. "For a guy that's getting what he wants, you sure do look sad."

Charles's hands hovered as he gripped the soldering iron. He frowned, trying to recapture his focus.

"Naturally," he said, "I shall be sad to say goodbye to all my new friends."

"Aw, thanks, buddy." Dan playfully kicked snow in Charles's direction.

Charles couldn't stop his smile. "But," he continued, "I will be quite happy to return to my own time. It's quieter, and slower."

"I didn't think you liked *quiet* or *slow*."

"Perhaps," Charles said, straightening, "I appreciate them more now. Thanks to you and your family."

"And Megan," Dan added with a pointed look.

"And Megan." Charles exhaled. Merely saying her name filled him with dueling emotions—joy and sorrow. It was lowering to think that, after tonight, he'd never speak her name again. "I wish I could celebrate Christmas with her."

Now that he'd said it aloud, he realized how true his words were. He felt none of his old dismissiveness of the holiday. In truth, the thought of a Christmas with Megan filled him with pleasure and expectation.

A picture arose in his mind with such clarity, it made his chest hurt: himself with Megan on Christmas morning, holding hands as they sat on the sofa in her parents' living room, surrounded by the scents of a delicious breakfast combined with the pine fragrance of the festive tree. There were mugs of cocoa and a fire burned cheerfully in the fireplace. Megan had her head on his shoulder while they watched her family excitedly open presents.

She'd given him a present that morning. Unwilling to part with it for even a few moments, he'd tucked it into the tool carrier.

Charles pulled the paper bag from the kit. It was cheerily decorated with bows, and its inside was filled with brightly hued tissue paper. *For: Charles, From: You Know Who!* was written on the bag in a feminine cursive.

He traced his finger over Megan's writing, picturing her with the pen in her hand.

"I'm not supposed to open this until I'm back home," he murmured, "and it's Christmas Day."

"But something tells me you can't wait."

"I built most of my fortune before I was twenty-one," Charles said. "Delaying things I want doesn't come easily to me. Besides," he added, "I have no guarantee that objects can travel through time with me, so it makes sense that I open it now."

Dan raised an eyebrow. "Better do some stretching so that you can be nice and warm for these mental acrobatics."

Charles shot his friend a look that said he didn't appreciate the sarcasm.

He reached into the gift bag and pulled out a book with a handsome leather cover. It had a tooled design of a vine that twisted and curved around the border, and, unlike many of the objects from this era, it appeared to be hand-crafted.

Opening it, he read *Charles's Christmas* on the front page.

He turned the page, and discovered photographs pasted on the pages, with Megan's handwriting beneath them. *Tree-Lighting Ceremony. Top of the Library. At the Theater. Funny Hat Party. Hula-Hoops!*

Looking closer, he saw that the photographs were of him, or him and Megan, enjoying the holiday together. She must have taken the pictures with her phone without him noticing, and perhaps some of the other images had been taken by members of her family. On some of the pages, she'd written descriptive paragraphs beside the photographs. She had also included things such as a ticket stub from Amber's performance of the holiday plays, a few needles from a pine tree, and a copy of her father's cookie recipe.

Charles stared at the journal, overcome. His breath left him completely and his heart thudded furiously. He felt as though he'd been hit with an I-beam—in a good way.

"Wow!" Dan exclaimed. "That's a really nice gift."

"It is," Charles said in a dazed voice. The world seemed to whirl around him, and he could barely hold on and keep from being flung into the ether.

"Looks like she made it herself," Dan said.

"It does. An extraordinary amount of work."

Dan gave Charles a look of understanding, and

patted him on the shoulder. "It'll make for a nice reminder of your time in the future."

"It's more than that." Charles closed the journal and held it snug against his chest. "It's a chronicle of the best days of my life."

She'd done that for him, given him a priceless gift.

She'd given him her heart, too, bravely offering it to him. Yet he'd had to return it. Though it had been necessary to do so, he could not forgive himself for hurting her so terribly. If circumstances had been different, he would have embraced that gift, and given his own heart in return.

It already belonged to her.

Here was his secret sorrow—he loved Megan.

A week was a short span of time, yet he'd lived a lifetime within it—because of her. With her generosity and her beautiful soul, she'd opened the world to him. He had only to look at her or hear her voice, and he was like a zeppelin rising high into the air. He lived for her happiness and success. And that's how he knew that he was in love with her, because he wanted nothing for himself and everything for her, and he recognized this selfless devotion for what it was.

But he had to tuck his feelings away and continue on with his plan to return home. They were from different worlds, he and Megan, each with their own paths to walk. His own time was full of things he longed to do, plans he wanted to realize. He couldn't walk away from all that. Could he?

He prayed that the journal would travel with him

back to his time. It had to. He couldn't part with it. Days and months and years would pass, and he would always have this record to return to again and again. Even when the pages faded and fell apart, he'd remember this time.

Forever.

Strange how, in such a short span of time, Charles had begun to feel at home in his modern clothing, and now his garments from 1902 felt like a costume.

As he slipped on his coat, he caught a glimpse of himself in the mirror hanging on the back of the bedroom door. Coat, waistcoat, high-collared shirt, necktie. The standard outfit for a gentleman of his era. No more T-shirts, or jeans.

He looked just as he had the night he had "disappeared," and yet inside, he felt completely different. The clothes themselves seemed constraining. They were too stiff, too formal. He certainly couldn't Hula-Hoop in this suit.

With longing, he looked toward the bag of clothes borrowed from Nathan Turner, which now sat at the foot of the bed. Earlier, he'd gone to something called a *laundromat*, and in the span of an hour, had been able to clean and dry everything. Miraculous. What Rosie and her staff would give to have access to such incredible machines.

But he'd have to resign himself to life without washing machines, and mobile telephones, and the ability to research a problem within less than a minute. There would be no pizza, no cars powered by electricity.

No Dan and Sophia, or Phillip, or Amber.

No Megan.

You belong back in 1902.

He'd been reminding himself of that all day as he'd completed his Christmas surprise. He was meant to return to his own era and reclaim the life that Harold Moran would steal from him if he didn't take action. That motivation had guided him all this week, propelling him forward to go back to the past. It wasn't *his* past, it was his future.

The cerebral gymnastics required for making sense of all this left him slightly dizzy. Yet it didn't matter. He'd correct the deviation of his life's course and get back to where he was supposed to be.

He slipped into his coat pocket the journal that Megan had made. It rather spoiled the line of the garment, making it hang a little strangely, but what did that matter? It would travel with him, come what may. He refused to part with it.

While Charles had finished his surprise for Megan earlier in the day, Dan had checked an almanac. The lunar eclipse would take place at fifteen minutes past eight o'clock in the evening.

Glancing at his pocket watch, Charles noted with a heavy heart that eight-fifteen was only thirty minutes away. Such a brief time left in this century, with the people who had grown so dear to him.

The mansion's Christmas Eve party had already begun. He was torn between the desire to hide himself away until the appointed time, and the need to spend every last moment with his friends. With Megan.

Protecting himself from hurt was a fool's errand. It would come whether he shut himself off or embraced his experience with open arms. Better, then, to move toward it rather than flee. So he would meet life head-on.

He hurried from his room to join the festivities.

Charles walked through the long corridors, following the sounds of music and laughter. It filled him with a bittersweet happiness to hear merriment here in his rather enormous house.

Charles emerged into the ballroom and smiled to see it packed with festively dressed visitors. A woman Phillip had referred to as a *DJ* stood at one end of the ballroom in front of two phonograph turntables— without the large horn that, in his day, was used to amplify sound. Instead, two large black cabinets covered with fabric flanked the DJ, and from them emanated buoyant holiday music.

People danced in couples and groups, including several adults dancing with children, and little boys and girls shaking sleigh bells as they hopped around on their own. Charles spotted Ali dancing with a pretty woman in a headscarf. He gave them a wave. Ali grinned and waved back, before returning to the dancing.

Moving out of the ballroom, Charles found the corridor full of guests enjoying the party.

"Hello, welcome," he murmured to visitors as he walked. "Welcome to my home. Merry Christmas."

He received many greetings in return, and his chest swelled with pride. The house looked beautiful with its holiday decorations, the air was rich with the scent of pine, and many happy voices joined together to form a river of sound. It felt wonderful to open his home to people and share in celebrating the season together.

When he returned to his time, he would make a point of entertaining more guests. Having the expansive space of his house filled with people enjoying themselves made him feel buoyant and light. Eliza had always enjoyed parties in Newport and in the Hamptons, so surely she would enjoy being a hostess in their home.

He would make certain that the mansion was always open to friends and guests, and filled with parties and celebrations and gatherings and *life*.

He would see Eliza again. Soon. While he felt the expectation of moving forward in his life, he searched for a feeling of warmth and connection with his fiancée. Yet his search was in vain. There was a shadowy outline in his heart where a vivacious, fully dimensional Eliza should have been. That would have to be remedied. She was a good person. She deserved someone who valued her, adored her, and lavished her with affection and respect.

Would she get that affection and respect from Moran? Perhaps she'd have a fulfilling marriage. Or perhaps she wouldn't. Charles's decision shaped many futures.

He entered the parlor and a poignant happiness burst in his chest as he saw Megan standing with Dan, Lydia, and Sophia. His friends. Charles possessed no camera, but he took a mental picture so that he could return to this memory many times.

"Merry Christmas," he said, with an effort at cheer.

"Merry Christmas," the Romano family answered in unison.

Megan smiled, but there was a distinct sorrow in her expression that couldn't be missed. "All set to go?"

"There are a few things to attend to first," he said, thinking of his surprise. He'd covered it with several tarps so that he could unveil it later. As to the depth of his feelings for her, those he couldn't share. It would only make his leaving all the more agonizing.

"Don't forget to tell Charles your good news," Dan said, nudging Megan.

"What good news?" Charles asked.

"I—"

"They want her to become a professor!" Sophia burst out.

Lydia chuckled. "Honey, you've got to let people speak for themselves."

The little girl turned red. "Sorry—I got excited."

"That's okay, Sophia," Megan said, placing her hand on the girl's shoulder. "I'm pretty excited, too."

"So it's true?" Charles asked. "They've given you the position?"

"Not exactly," Megan said. "I'm going in next week to interview."

Elation rose up in Charles, cutting through his gloom. Everything she wanted was coming to pass, and he couldn't imagine a better outcome. "That's wonderful, Megan! Congratulations."

He moved to embrace her, then stopped. Instead, he kept his arms at his sides. The less he held her, the easier leaving her might be—though he doubted anything could make this easier. How did you simply walk away from the person you love?

"Are we sharing good news?" Amber asked, rushing forward. She radiated excitement, and practically bounced on her feet like a child.

"We are," Megan said.

"I got an email from the producers." Amber looked at each of them, holding onto a dramatic pause. Fitting. "I got a callback!"

The small group all cried out together. Megan swooped in and hugged Amber as Sophia and Lydia clapped their hands.

"That's amazing!" Megan rocked Amber from side to side. "I knew you could do it."

"Not so fast! A callback doesn't mean they're casting me."

"But they will."

"Thank you," Amber said. "For everything." She pulled back enough to smile widely at all of them. "They want me in New York on January second."

"We'll have to recast the part of Eliza," Megan said.

Amber wrinkled up her nose apologetically. "Maybe!"

"But my dad can play Charles," Sophia said, "when he goes."

A quiet fell on the group. Charles hated seeing the look of sorrow on Megan's face. It tore him from the inside out. Yet his path was clear—he had to return home.

Phillip approached, wearing a red-and-green sweater that could be modestly described as *gaudy*. Charles's eyes ached to behold it.

"What's this I hear about losing not just my Charles, but possibly also Eliza?" he asked.

"Sorry, Phillip," Amber said, contrite.

But Phillip smiled. "I'm not! This is an amazing opportunity, and you can't let it slip by."

"Even if I don't get the role, thanks so much for giving me a place to hone my skills. I'm lucky to have this job."

Phillip waved that compliment away. "You won't need your job here much longer. Besides, we were the lucky ones. Just remember to give the museum a shout-out when you're accepting your Tony Award." He turned to Charles. "We're going to miss you here, too."

"As I will miss everyone." But Charles's gaze was solely on Megan as he spoke. He couldn't look anywhere else.

Until Phillip coughed theatrically, drawing everyone's attention. "Are you ready for the Istmaschray

Urprisesay?" he asked with a wink that was so obvious it could have been spotted from Canada.

Despite the sadness in her eyes, Megan laughed. "You missed your calling as an international man of mystery, Phillip."

"Agent Double-O Obvious, that's me."

Charles had no idea what Phillip meant with that comment, but everyone chuckled, so he permitted himself a small smile.

"Regardless of his subtle handling," he said, "there's something outside that I would very much enjoy showing everyone." He raised his voice so he could be heard throughout the room. "If all the guests could gather on the front lawn, they'll get a chance to see a little holiday treat from Charles Whitley, himself."

"And," Phillip added, "before the reveal, Mr. Whitley has a few things to say."

Charles whipped his head around to stare at Phillip. "He does?"

The man had the gall to look innocent. "Oh, didn't I tell you? Charles Whitley always gives a speech at the Christmas party."

"You most certainly did *not* tell me." A light film of sweat clung to his back. Oh, he could address his board of directors with little difficulty. At the prospect of speaking to at least a hundred people, however, his mouth went dry.

"You don't have to do or say anything you don't want to," Megan said firmly. "Phillip can give the speech."

Warmth stole through Charles at her defense of him.

"Hey," Amber said, "if it helps, there are no consequences. After tonight, you're not going to see any of these people ever again."

Oddly, that did lift the pressure that threatened to crush him. "Thank you, Amber." Considering it, he saw that gave him the freedom to say whatever he liked, to speak truly and from the heart. He wouldn't get the opportunity again.

"I believe I shall address the guests," he said after a moment.

"Great!" Phillip said, clapping his hands together.

Murmuring with excitement and interest, the guests gathered and started moving outside. Amber, Lydia, Sophia, Dan, and Phillip joined the exodus.

Excitement, nervousness, and anticipation knotted in Charles's belly as he turned to Megan. Not only would he speak to the crowd, but he also had his surprise for her. He prayed she'd like it.

He held out his arm.

"Would you accompany me, Miss Turner?"

There was the briefest pause before she said, "I would be delighted, Mr. Whitley." She took his arm.

The sensation of her hand on him set off internal fireworks. He tried to hold on to the sensation—he'd never experience it again.

They walked out together—for the last time.

CHAPTER NINETEEN

Moving with the crowd, Megan walked with Charles outside. Despite her unhappiness over Charles's imminent departure, she smiled to see how the front lawn of the mansion had been transformed into a winter wonderland.

Light-draped booths had been set up by Tina's crew of caterers, offering grilled meat on skewers, cider and cocoa, and apple hand pies. The long lines moved quickly as the staff operated efficiently, and people clustered in groups happily munched on their food.

Not everyone was eating. Other booths were arranged on the lawn, including games of ring-around-the-bottle, bean bag tossing, and snow golf putting. Theater students from the university painted kids' faces to look like reindeer or snowmen, and there was also a photo booth, complete with a prop Santa and elf hats for goofy poses, along with a nearby sign that read *#WhitleyMoranChristmas*.

Children played tag and threw snowballs, with an

occasional adult joining in the fun. A few people had brought dogs, adorably costumed in plaid jackets or big red bows. Megan waved at Mr. Burgess and his two pets, one dressed as Santa, the other in an elf costume.

Garlands and lights everywhere made the whole scene sparkle. The music from inside was piped out onto the lawn, and scattered fire pits added warmth.

It was a picture-perfect holiday scene, and Megan and Charles stopped to take it all in.

"What a glorious sight," Charles said softly as the Christmas lights shone in his eyes.

"Every year, it gets better and better. This year might be the best yet." But it was also the hardest to bear.

She looked up, and he did, too. They both stared at the full red moon overhead.

It wouldn't be long, now.

Her stomach pitched to somewhere around her feet.

"Are you all set for your speech?" Phillip asked as he approached.

"I'm ready," Charles said, and he slipped his arm out from beneath her hand.

She missed the feel of him immediately.

Charles walked in front of something covered with a huge tarp. He swept the tarp aside, revealing a large mechanical contraption that looked as though it had been assembled from a mixture of old and new technology. Megan recognized a few parts, such as pistons, cylinders, coupling rods, and LED screens, but most of it was beyond her limited technical knowledge.

What on Earth *was* this?

Charles coughed nervously into his fist, but then he glanced in her direction. She smiled encouragingly, giving him a reassuring nod. At her smile, his posture changed, growing taller and straighter. In the glow from the Christmas lights, dressed impeccably in his custom-made suit, he'd never looked more handsome.

She savored the sight. For a moment, she thought to take a picture of him, then discarded the idea. This night, with all its sadness, would live in her memory alone.

Charles raised his arms and spread them out, signaling for quiet.

The crowd hushed. Everyone waited in anticipation—including Megan. She'd seen the terror on Charles's face when Phillip had sprung the speech on him. It appeared that public speaking wasn't something Charles was familiar with. No doubt he had nothing prepared, so it would have to be entirely spontaneous.

Though she felt nervous for him, she had every confidence that he'd think of the right things to say.

"Friends," he said in a voice that carried across the lawn, "I welcome you to my home so that we may share the joys of the season together." His expression shifted, becoming thoughtful. "I used to disdain the holiday. It was a lot of flash and noise, but meant almost nothing to me."

Unsettled murmurs arose from the crowd, not sure

how to interpret this remark. Megan fought to keep from grimacing. She hoped he was going somewhere with this train of thought.

He continued, "It took something extraordinary to learn how very wrong I was."

Megan tensed. He wasn't *really* going to talk about traveling through time, was he?

"I met some remarkable people," he said, "and they were kind enough to give me the gift of friendship." He nodded at Dan, Lydia, Sophia, Amber, and Phillip, and also at a bearded man Megan thought she recognized from the post office. Charles's eyes gleamed with warmth and affection.

"Through them, I learned the value of this season. Togetherness, closeness, generosity of spirit. Spending time with people you care about. They cannot be placed beneath a tree to open on Christmas morning, but when these gifts are given to us, we carry them with us forever. And I wouldn't have known any of that, were it not for my friends."

Coolness touched Megan's cheeks, and she realized that tears trailed down her face. She didn't wipe them away, wanting to fully feel this moment rather than hide from her emotions.

"I want everyone here to promise me one thing," Charles went on. "Tomorrow morning, I want you to turn to the people you love, and give them the gift of your heart. Tell them how much you care about them. Tell them that you respect and value them. Tell them that no matter what, no matter what distance or time separates you, you will always be there for them. That you will never, ever forget them."

He said these last words to her alone.

Megan's tears fell faster now. Dimly, she felt Amber's arm wrap around her shoulders, but all her focus was on Charles. He looked at her as if she was the entire world.

For the rest of her life, she'd remember this feeling, when elation and sadness lived side by side within her, bathing her in light and darkening her with shadow.

He blinked furiously before clearing his throat again.

"And now, friends, I have a small gift for all of you—though I admit, I created it for one person in particular." His gaze sped to her before he busied himself with a wooden box with a lever. "Sophia, will you do the honors?"

Excitedly, the little girl ran up and gripped the lever. She looked up at Charles, waiting for his signal. When he nodded, she pulled the lever.

With a hiss and a rumble, the device began to work. The pistons chugged up and down and the coupling rods rotated. All of the guests pressed forward to watch as the mystery contraption clanged to life.

Suddenly, lights all over the machine blazed in a beautiful display. They had been arranged to form the shapes of trees, snowflakes, and bells. But they were animated so that the trees waved back and forth, the snowflakes fell, and the bells chimed. A miniature calliope began to play "God Rest Ye Merry

Gentlemen," while the LED screens showed images of dancers in turn-of-the-century clothing, moving in time with the music.

It was the most spectacular thing Megan had ever seen.

The crowd burst into applause, and everyone whipped out their phones to record it. Without a doubt, the videos of the display would go viral, and for good reason.

"Oh my goodness, Charles!" Megan turned to him. "Did you make this?"

He looked almost abashed as he said, "I had help from Dan, Amber, and Phillip in financing it. But yes, I did design and build it. It's my Christmas gift to you."

"I…" Her eyes filled with tears of joy and sadness. How was it possible for a person to feel such conflicting emotions all at once? "It's the most incredible gift I've ever received. Thank you."

He opened his mouth as if to speak, but no words came. They were both bathed with light, standing beside each other wordlessly, while all around them, guests and staff celebrated the holiday.

If only this moment could last forever.

But it ended when Dan approached them, holding Sophia's hand.

"Guys," he said, his voice gentle, "it's time."

Megan let out a breath. There was no delaying the inevitable. Maybe it was better to be done with so she could start healing the wound that would come with the loss of Charles.

"Want to say goodbye to Amber and Phillip?" she asked.

"I just want to get this over with." He bared his teeth. "Not because I want to leave, but because… because…" He shook his head. "Because."

She understood.

Silently, she followed Charles into the house, while Dan and Sophia trailed after them. They wove through the guests that had returned inside. Suddenly, the festive atmosphere felt oppressive, and Megan longed to run outside and fill her lungs with cold air. But she wouldn't flee, so she kept going, following Charles as he entered his study.

It was quiet in the room, the sounds of revelry muted. Sitting on the desk in readiness was the clock. To Megan's eyes, it looked enormous and ominous, though it hadn't truly changed. It was the same broken device it had always been—except now they had the means to repair it. And to activate its special powers.

It was so strange that this one, fairly ordinary object could change the course of a human life. But here it was, offering Charles a chance to return to his era.

He faced Dan and Sophia.

"You've done so much for me," he said. "Both of you. You've given me the kind of friendship I've never truly had before, and I thank you for it."

"It's an honor to be your friend," Dan said.

Charles held out his hand.

For a moment, Dan just looked at Charles's offered

hand. Then, muttering, "Ah, the heck with it," he took hold of Charles's wrist and pulled him close for a manly embrace.

Charles was briefly frozen, then he returned the hug.

Watching it all, Megan pressed her fingertips to her trembling lips with her other hand resting on Sophia's shoulder.

Dan slapped Charles's back. "Take care of yourself, buddy."

"And you do the same," Charles said. "You're blessed with a wonderful family."

"Don't I know it."

The two men broke apart with slightly embarrassed chuckles.

Charles crouched down so that he was eye level with Sophia. Megan could feel the little girl's body shake as she struggled to hold back tears.

"Do you have to go?" Sophia said quietly, breaking Megan's heart.

"I'm sorry, sweetheart," Charles said, his voice kind. "I do. But I want you to know how special you are. I know you're going to change the world." From his waistcoat, he produced a pocket watch. "I bought this for myself when I registered my first patent." He held it out to her.

"For me?" Sophia's eyes were huge.

Charles nodded solemnly. "So you can remember how precious time is, and to take each minute as a gift."

"Thank you." Sophia carefully took the watch from Charles and held it tightly in her small fist.

Charles straightened to face Megan. She wanted, more than anything, to beg him to stay. She wanted, more than anything, to run as far as she could and not face this moment. But she couldn't do either. She needed to be right here, with him, until the very end.

"Megan—"

"Oh, Charles." She wasn't sure she could survive his goodbye.

He stroked the backs of his fingers down her cheek. "Perhaps you could come with me."

Her heart throbbed, the pain nearly overwhelming her.

"You know I can't," she said.

"I do," he answered. "But I wanted to try, just the same."

She sniffed. "*You* were my Christmas present."

He ducked his head. "I couldn't wait, and I opened your gift." Emotion shone in his eyes. "Thank you. For opening my heart. I shall miss you for the rest of my days."

"I'll miss you, too." She dashed her knuckles across her eyes, trying to stop the flow of tears. "But now it's time for you to go home, and live the life you were meant to have."

As one, they moved, and wrapped their arms around each other. She held onto him tightly, soaking in the feel of him, drawing his scent into her lungs. The pain might one day lessen, but for now, she'd hold it near, because it meant she had given her heart to someone who deserved her love.

He pressed his cheek against the top of her head. A tremor shook his whole body, and then, with what seemed like a titanic effort, he pulled away.

He went to the window, and Megan followed. The black disk of the Earth's shadow began to slide across the moon.

The time had come.

Charles approached the clock as one might approach the edge of a cliff. He drew in a deep breath and pulled out the missing piece. He moved to put the piece back into place.

"Might I do this alone?" he asked. "It would be easier for me."

"Of course," Megan said. Even though she wouldn't be with him until the very end, she had to honor his needs.

Dan and Sophia headed toward the door to the study. Megan followed, though she couldn't stop herself from looking over her shoulder. Finally, she crossed the threshold, pulling the door shut behind her.

"Should we go?" Sophia asked.

"Let's give it a minute, honey," Dan said.

Megan spread her hand over the wood, as if she could will her spirit into the study so that it could have these last moments with Charles.

The next time she opened the door, the study would be empty, and Charles would be gone.

A moment passed. She wasn't certain when to go in. Maybe if she postponed it, she wouldn't have to accept it as true.

She jumped when a loud crash sounded from inside the study. It sounded like something mechanical being smashed to pieces.

Fearing that something terrible had happened to Charles, she flung the door open and raced inside. Dan and Sophia followed her.

Charles was still there. At his feet lay the broken parts of the clock. It had exploded everywhere into tiny fragments—too small to ever be reassembled—as though someone had thrown it violently to the ground.

"Oh, no!" Sophia cried. She immediately dropped to her knees and began to gather up the pieces.

"Don't bother, Sophia," Charles said. The expression on his face was serene, utterly at peace.

Realization hit Megan. Charles had deliberately destroyed the clock.

His gaze found Megan's and didn't budge. "I'm staying."

She gasped, as did Dan.

"What?" she exclaimed. Her heart raced and she could barely keep standing.

Charles approached her, his face filled with joy. "You taught me how to enjoy life in the present moment. I cannot imagine a future—in any century—without you."

She felt as though she'd been flung high up into the sky, only to discover she had grown wings. Never had she experienced such all-encompassing happiness.

He was staying. *Staying*. For her. For *them*.

The passage of time folded in on itself. She only knew that one moment, she stood on her own in the study, and the next, Charles was kissing her. It was such a lovely kiss, full of love and happiness.

It was made all the better knowing that it didn't mean goodbye. It was merely the beginning.

"Daddy," Sophia whispered loudly, "we should give them some privacy."

"Oh!" Dan said. "Right!"

Megan and Charles briefly broke apart, unable to stop their laughter.

"Merry Christmas," Charles said to Dan and Sophia.

"Merry Christmas," the father and daughter answered back.

Maybe Dan and Sophia left the study. Maybe they stayed. Megan couldn't be certain, because all she saw was Charles. The way he was looking at her, too, it was reasonable to assume that all he saw was her.

They had truly received the greatest gift of all.

EPILOGUE

One year later...

Megan hurried up the steps of Tina's Diner, swinging her briefcase full of student papers and humming a few bars of "God Rest Ye Merry Gentlemen."

She pushed open the door and warmth gusted over her, along with the scents of lemongrass and ginger. Traditional Christmas music played on the sound system. From behind the counter, Tina gave Megan a wave. Megan waved back, but didn't stop, heading toward one booth in particular.

"Hey there," she said with a smile to Charles, sliding into the seat opposite him.

He pushed aside the laptop on which he'd been working, his own smile wide.

It didn't matter how many times she saw that smile, it never failed to make her pulse beat faster.

"Why hello, most brilliant of all history lecturers."

He reached across the table and took her hand. The sensation of his skin against hers thrilled and calmed her at the same time. "How did teaching go today?"

"Amazing," she said without hesitation. "My students are so enthusiastic. Half of them turned their papers in early because they were so eager to write them."

She'd been teaching an Introduction to American History course for two semesters at the university, and while the work load was considerable, she couldn't complain about it. Not when she was doing exactly what she loved. Sure, there were minor irritations, and she was learning her way through the academic bureaucracy, yet these concerns were small compared to the sense of fulfillment she got every day going to work.

"Oh, and I got a text from Amber," she said. "The touring company is in London now, and she's having the best time."

"Capital!"

They'd found talented history buffs to play both Eliza as well as Rosie, since neither Amber nor Megan worked at the mansion any more. Attendance was better than ever, according to the email she'd gotten from Phillip, and this year, for the annual Christmas party, they planned on using Charles's incredible display again, which was sure to draw many more visitors.

"What about you?" she asked. "How was your day?"

"Dan sent me a selfie." Charles showed her the screen on her phone, and she saw Dan dressed as "Charles Whitley," surrounded by smiling visitors. Dan had grown in his beard to make sure he played the role as accurately as possible. He looked utterly content, having finally secured the part he'd wanted for so long.

"And," Charles continued, "I have some good news."

Megan waited expectantly.

"All the work I've been doing as a history consultant for film productions—I've been saving my wages. Now I finally have enough capital to start up that business you and I have been talking about. Take a look."

He spun his laptop around, revealing a fun but elegant website splash page for Past Perfect. It featured photographs of beautifully made machines from the early twentieth century, including small steam engines, sewing machines, adding machines, and typewriters. For almost a year, Charles had been in touch with artisanal manufacturers all across the East Coast, sending pictures and ideas back and forth as they developed the machines that they intended to sell to living history centers, museums, and collectors. The gorgeous machines were all made of polished brass and sustainably harvested wood, and would be built to order.

Megan felt a touch of giddiness to see all of Charles's hard work finally coming to fruition. They both had worked very hard to make this happen for him.

"That's wonderful, Charles!"

"The website went live this morning," he said eagerly, "and I've already received orders from New York, Dallas, Tokyo, and Sao Paulo."

"I'm so happy for you." She squeezed his hand.

Adapting to the modern world was sometimes bumpy—they were still trying to figure out how to curtail his online shopping—but he'd adjusted brilliantly, just as she'd known he would.

"That's not everything I have been working on," Charles said. He fidgeted with the salt and pepper shakers, and kept glancing to the side, his gaze restless.

Was it her imagination, or did he suddenly seem very nervous?

"Shall I show you?" he asked.

"Please."

He tapped a few buttons on his computer, and the website disappeared, replaced by a collage.

Pictures appeared on the screen, and she recognized them as the photos she and Charles had taken throughout the year: toasting the New Year beside the fireplace at her parents' house, hugging in front of a Valentine's Day display of roses, posing with their sand castle at the beach, wearing star-spangled hats as fireworks shot into the air behind them, and carving pumpkins on the front steps of her parents' house. A year's worth of amazing adventures with Charles. Just seeing them again filled her with rosy happiness, and she felt a profound gratitude to whoever had made that now-broken clock send Charles into the future.

Words materialized on the screen of Charles's laptop: *LOOK UP.*

She did, and her mouth dropped open when she saw him beside the booth on one knee.

"Miss Megan Turner," he said, his voice strong even as it shook with emotion, "you have given me more incredible experiences in a year than I'd had in the entirety of my life. I can't wait to see what we do next, or where we'll go. Will you marry me?"

She fought for breath, the room tilting on its axis. She tried to speak, but her ability to form words beyond *guh* seemed to have disappeared.

"Say yes!"

Megan jumped at the sound of Sophia's voice. She looked around the diner and saw now that the booths were all filled with the people she cared about most: Dan, Sophia, Lydia, Phillip, her mom and dad, and Nathan and Elena with their baby daughter. Tina stood nearby, an image of Amber on her phone's screen as she watched via video chat from faraway London.

Everyone wore matching expressions of nervous expectation.

Tears ran down her cheeks, but she didn't pay any attention. All that mattered right then was Charles, apprehensively waiting for her answer.

Finally, she managed to speak.

"Yes, Charles."

"Yes?"

"Yes!"

The sounds of applause and cheers filled the air, yet her awareness was only of Charles, who had swept her up in his arms to give her a heart-stopping kiss.

"Megan," he whispered against her lips, "I can't wait for us to spend the future together."

She would have answered him, saying that she felt the same way, but she was too overcome. Pleasure and happiness and contentment spun and swirled within her. She couldn't find words, only feelings. So she kissed him again.

Somehow, through the strangest quirk of fate as time had braided together, she and Charles had found each other. And they were never letting go.

The End

STUFFED CRUST ITALIAN PIZZA

A Hallmark Original Recipe

In *A Timeless Christmas*, Charles Whitley—a man who's traveled forward in time from 1902—has never heard of pizza. Megan has to explain to him that it's okay to eat it with his hands. After the first bite, he declares it's the best thing he's ever tasted. Charles would've been even more impressed by our Stuffed Crust Italian Pizza. It's a few steps up from delivery pizza, and perfect any time.

Yield: 1 12-inch pizza (4 servings)
Prep Time: 20 minutes
Bake Time: 15 minutes

INGREDIENTS

- 1 (16 oz.) ball refrigerated pizza dough, at room temperature
- 8 mozzarella string cheese sticks, at room temperature
- ½ cup pizza sauce
- 2 cups shredded mozzarella cheese
- 12 slices pepperoni
- ½ medium-size red bell pepper, seeded and cut into ¼-inch-thick slices
- 8 oz. bulk Italian pork sausage, cooked, drained, crumbled
- ½ cup cooked bacon, 1-inch dice
- 2 tablespoons sliced, drained black olives
- as needed, grated Parmesan cheese
- as needed, chopped fresh parsley

DIRECTIONS

1. Preheat oven to 475°F. Coat a large pizza pan lightly with olive oil or cooking spray.

2. On a lightly floured surface, roll the dough out into a 14-inch round. Transfer to pizza pan.

3. Arrange string cheese sticks evenly in a 12-inch-wide circle over dough, leaving a

1-inch border around outer edge of dough. Fold outer edges of dough over string cheese and press to seal, forming a cheese stuffed pizza crust.

4. Spoon pizza sauce evenly over pizza dough; top with shredded cheese, pepperoni slices, bell pepper rings, crumbled sausage, diced bacon and black olives.

5. Bake for 12 to 15 minutes, or until crust is golden and cheese is bubbly. Remove from oven.

6. Garnish pizza with grated Parmesan cheese and chopped parsley. Cut into 8 slices.

Thanks so much for reading *A Timeless Christmas*. We hope you enjoyed it!

You might like these other books from Hallmark Publishing:

The Christmas Company
Christmas in Evergreen
A Christmas to Remember
Journey Back to Christmas
Love You Like Christmas
A Heavenly Christmas

For information about our new releases and exclusive offers, sign up for our free newsletter at hallmarkchannel.com/hallmark-publishing-newsletter

You can also connect with us here:

Facebook.com/HallmarkPublishing

Twitter.com/HallmarkPublish